THE INITIATES

Liminal Books

THE INITIATES

A Terrafide Novel

Ryan Hyatt

To Sage.

This one's for the youth.

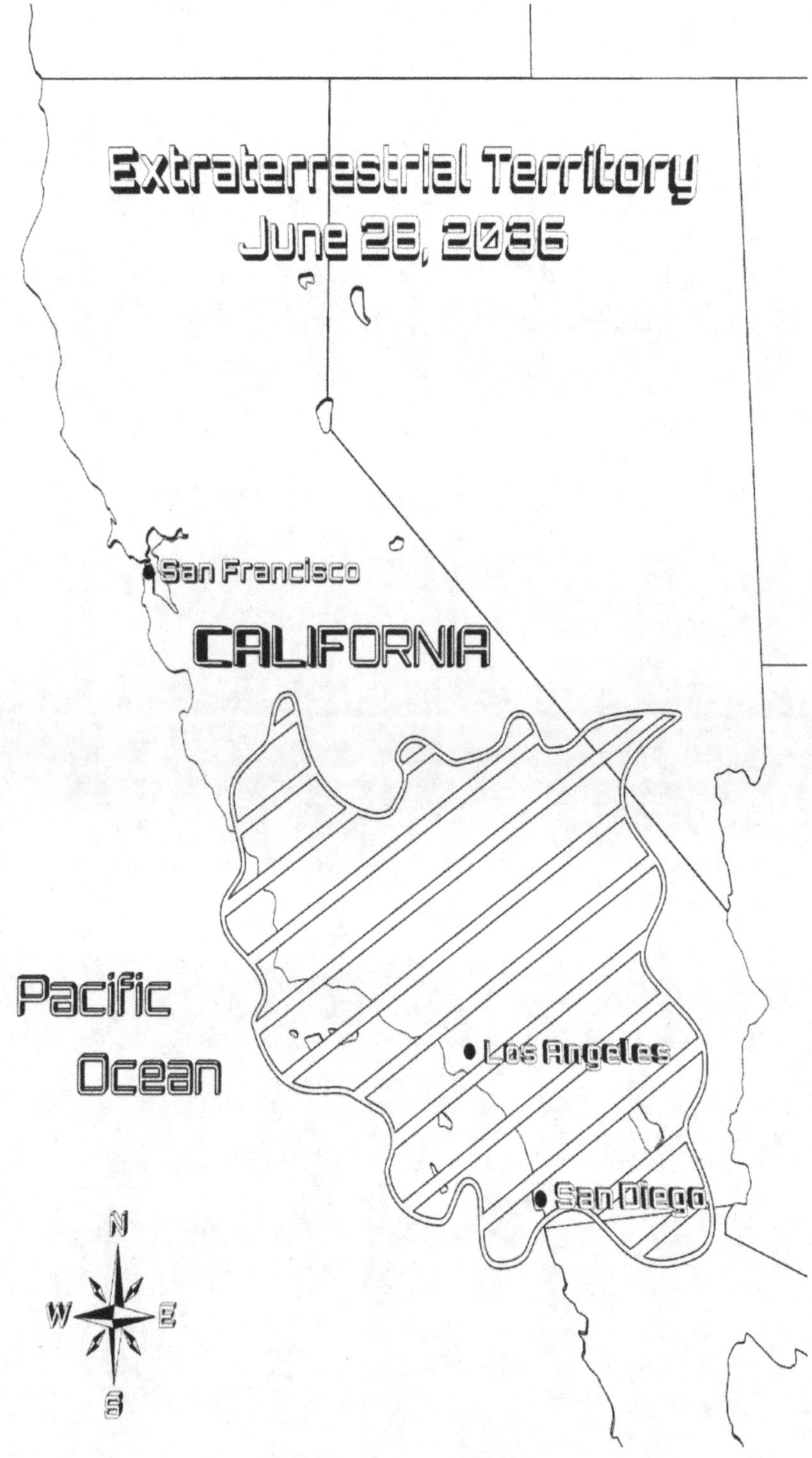

Extraterrestrial Territory
June 28, 2036
San Francisco
CALIFORNIA
Pacific
Ocean
Los Angeles
San Diego
N
W
E
S

Part 1

They Come from the Kiaski Nebula

Chapter 1

Graduating from high school is not the victory Myles hoped.

The exhilaration of watching hundreds of ceremonial caps tossed into the air, the thrill of knowing that he is no longer required to pledge allegiance to the flag, sit at a desk, and listen to a barrage of teachers drone on about covalent bonds, the French Revolution, and the 'habits of success' necessary for him to become a master of his destiny … dissolves into dread. A string of parties to celebrate liberation from institutionalized learning leaves Myles languishing in bed with the realization that he has no plan to replace the routine of school with a path toward gainful employment that will get him out of his mom's house and on with his life.

Knock, knock.

"Nobody's home," Myles whimpers, wrapping Supernova Cid around his head. The doll's soft stomach covers his eyes, preventing him from confronting what awaits beyond the bedroom door. He hears a growl, mistakes it for a monster, and realizes it's the grumbling of his stepfather's stomach.

"Go away," Myles mumbles. "We have enough Girl Scout cookies."

"You lie," counters a baritone voice. "You can never have enough Girl Scout cookies. Open up."

Despite the best efforts of Myles's teachers—who urged him to achieve his full potential, be all he can be, and live his best life—the overall impression for graduates like himself is that the responsibility foisted upon them—to save the planet and the future—is an impossible task. A terrifying joke, really. *The best we should hope for is a cataclysmic event, like the asteroid that killed the dinosaurs, to put us out of our collective misery.*

The door swings open.

"Breakfast is ready," his stepfather says, standing in his well-worn robe.

"Nooooo, Al …" Myles moans, but not even Supernova Cid can save him. He tosses the doll at his stepfather, who catches it in the air and holds it up high.

"Come on, Myles!" Al says, imitating the high-pitched voice of the childhood companion. "I'm not leaving … until you join me!"

The only thing worse for Myles than being paralyzed with post-high school existential fear is having his stepfather lording over him while he is paralyzed with post-high school existential fear. Myles wishes he had the strength and fortitude of Al, but in his bones, he feels more like his deadbeat dad.

"Fine," Myles mumbles to himself, rolling out of bed.

Al tosses Supernova Cid onto the pillow and closes the door. Three days into graduation revelry, and the 18-year-old is dragged into the kitchen, directed to sit at the table, and presented with his stepfather's perspective on the state of human affairs.

"It's simple," Al says, filling a mug with coffee, handing it to his stepson. "You can stay here as long as you'd like, Myles, but you will need to start paying for room and board, just like you would anywhere else you live. Welcome to the way the world works."

At least school prepared Myles for arguments like this, he realizes as he sips the bitter black fuel. "The Great Pacific Garbage Patch is three times the size of Texas, and it keeps growing, with no end in sight. This continues to be the case, no matter how low the unemployment rate is or how well the stock market is doing. In other words, Al, the world does *not* work."

"You know that kind of idealism won't get you anywhere, right?"

"Greta seems to be doing fine."

"The climate activist? I wonder if she still lives at home, too."

Myles glares at his stepfather from behind his mug.

"I'm just saying, sometimes special people get special treatment," Al says, handing Myles a tablet. "Unfortunately, you're not one of them. You're too young to be moping around here with an old-timer like me. You graduated from high school. Great! Now it's time to figure out your next step."

The tablet is opened to an employment site.

"Juliet," Myles says, skimming the help wanted ads. "Resort poolside playlist, please."

The home computer selects a reggae tune as Al mumbles something about Myles's life *always* being a vacation.

Scouring the ads, the young man finds no shortage of uninspiring entry-level work. Barista, customer service rep, telemarketer—the list of companies in need of wage slaves to contribute to an unsustainable economy goes on forever, it seems. Still, one position catches Myles's eye:

COUNSELOR WANTED

Are you a positive role model? Do you have tenacity, grit, and a growth mindset? If so, we'd like to talk to you about providing high-quality educational and recreational experiences to children ages 8 to 14. 'Tis the season to make memories!

Sincerely,

Camp Friendly Forest

Myles stares at the company logo: smiling trees with branches clasping each other in a warm embrace. He searches for the location. Apparently, this cult in need of recruits is based in the Sierras, north of Los Angeles, far from his parents, where the higher altitude and cooler climes might make summer bearable. If he can ignore the camp's creepy rainbow-and-lollypops vibe, it's possible to imagine how escaping to the mountains and working as a counselor during the hottest months of the year might be sufferable. Hell, it may even be fun. After all, according to the movies and TV shows Myles streams, attractive ladies his age are known to loiter around wilderness communes.

"You're right, Al," Myles says, gazing at his stepfather's dark skin, starting to crack with age. "Maybe my life isn't over yet. Maybe there's something to look forward to besides the climate apocalypse."

"Glad the coffee is clearing your head."

But there's a catch: *I'm not sure I qualify as the 'positive role model' Camp Friendly Forest is looking for.* Myles crunches on a mouthful of oats and mulls over the conundrum. *If they invite me for an interview, I'll put on my pink Polo shirt and khakis and play the part of a hardworking, upbeat, natural-born leader. The fine folks at Camp Friendly Forest won't be able to resist hiring me!*

Myles points at the ad.

"That one," he says as if choosing a flavor of ice cream.

Al glances at the tablet and carries his empty bowl to the kitchen. "I always wanted to go to camp. Unfortunately, my mother raised me by herself, and she couldn't afford to send me." He loads the bowl into the dishwasher. "They'll cover your room and board and pay you, too? Sounds like a great opportunity."

A virtual interview leads to a job offer, which leads to a fingerprint and background check. Myles passes, and the message from Camp Friendly

Forest seems clear: *No creeps allowed, but people who interview in pink Polo shirts and khakis? Sure. Just don't force our guests to eat sugar-free smores.*

By the end of the week, the young man leaves his parent's house, lugging a duffel bag filled with essentials: puffer vest with multiple pockets, phone/charger, razor, sunblock, shades, shorts, socks, hip-hop T-shirts, underwear, toothbrush, water bottle, and Swiss Army knife. Also, a sleeping bag and pillow.

"They'll provide the rest," Myles assures Mom and Al.

"Not so fast," Mom says, unable to conceal her curiosity. She points to the ground. Myles rolls his eyes and plops his duffel bag on the driveway, and she conducts a last-minute spot-check on her son's packing.

"Are you sure you want to take *this*?" she asks, withdrawing Supernova Cid, her eyebrows forming peaks of suspicion.

"Be careful with that!" Myles says, removing the doll from her clasp.

Al shakes his head. "Your mom's got a point, Myles. Why don't you leave your teddy bear at home?"

Myles lays the doll on top of the heap of clothes in his duffel bag. "No way! It's one of a kind. I figured I'd show it off to the kids in my cabin, maybe give it to one of them as a prize for good behavior."

"Strange," Mom says, "I thought I threw it away years ago—"

A faded green van with the company name in white letters – *Camp Friendly Forest* – and the tree-hugging logo pulls up to the driveway.

Myles zips up the duffel bag, slings it around his shoulder. "That's my ride."

Mom, stepfather, and Myles hug each other goodbye.

"Good luck, Mr. Harper," Al says with a wink.

"Love you," Myles says to Mom, climbing aboard the van. *So much for high school,* he realizes as the vehicle peels away. *Adulting has begun.*

The route winds hundreds of miles north of Los Angeles and ends at a dusty lot at an altitude of 6,000 feet. A quick scan of the terrain includes one-story cabins scattered among clusters of boulders and groves of mighty redwood trees. Mission accomplished! Myles plans on finding a hammock and retiring immediately, but there's no bed in sight. Instead, he spots an amphitheater, archery field, basketball and tennis courts, pool—all signs of intense human activity.

Maybe this summer won't be a picnic.

A brunette with freckles exits a building labeled *Trading Post*, her curvy body bursting from a tank top and shorts, arms loaded with chips and soda. She nods. Myles waves back.

Sweet! Camp Friendly Forest has a convenience store with enough junk food to get us through a zombie apocalypse.

"Glad you made it, Mr. Harper."

Myles turns and finds a tall, chiseled fellow with shaggy blond hair and a TV-host grin. A fully developed man with broad shoulders. Old enough to buy alcohol, at least, maybe rent a car. Myles recognizes him from his interview.

"Geo?"

"In the flesh," Geo says with a smile that doesn't flinch. "You'll be handling Cabin 5, *Whispering Dreams*," he explains, glancing at a clipboard, pointing one direction. "Orientation starts in the dining hall in an hour." He points in another direction, still grinning. "The fun starts tomorrow."

"Yes ... sir," Myles says, scampering away.

The first-time camp counselor wanders among dull cinder-block buildings until he finds *Whispering Dreams*, identified by name and a '5' painted on the door. Myles stops to contemplate the creepy, sprawling mural spread across the side wall: a sweeping green pasture filled with birds, butterflies, cows, flowers, a unicorn, and rainbow, with a silver U.F.O. peeking down from clouds above.

Camp Friendly Forest really is a cult.

Inside the cabin, *Whispering Dreams* is lined with hard bunks sure to provide little rest for a band of zealot minors and the poor counselor assigned to supervise them. Myles plops his duffel bag on the bottom bed, closest to the exit, and glances across the breezeway at the adjoining cabin. *Passionate Pursuits*, door slightly open, is occupied by a Latin dude with a mullet squatting on a bunk listening to music.

"The girls I went to school with obsessed over this song," Myles says, sitting across from the fellow as the popular tune, 'Heartbreak Street,' plays on a boombox. "They used to blast it at lunch."

"I wouldn't know much about that," says the dude, eyeing his visitor sideways. "I stopped attending high school after my freshman year."

"Why?"

"I got kicked out."

Myles's mouth won't stay shut. "And they hired you to work *here*? With *kids*?"

"That was a long time ago," the dude says with a smirk. "I graduated online. I'm part of the Community Youth Corps. You know, one of those do-gooder government programs." He shuts off the boombox, stands, and lingers by the door. "I made mistakes—mistakes I've learned from. One more summer without any problems, and I can start working in the schools and helping youngsters who struggle like I did. Those who are staying in my cabin are from my part of town. Here on a grant."

"I see," Myles says, following him outside. "Good for you."

"Good for *them*," he says, hands in the air, marveling at the scenery. "I never went any place cool like this when I was a kid. Most I ever got to do living in East L.A. was attend a picnic at a park with a dirty pond surrounded by homeless people."

"I hear you," Myles says, extending his hand. "I'm from West Hollywood, and my parents didn't even bother taking me to the park. If we couldn't play a game in the front yard, we didn't play at all. Myles Harper."

"José Rodriguez," José says, slapping Myles's hand. "I hope you're ready, homie, cuz this summer … is gonna be lit."

Chapter 2

No luck daydreaming in a hammock. Myles's arrival at Camp Friendly Forest spurs a whirlwind of exertion, beginning with a tour of the fifty-acre facility.

Geo leads the Angeleno and sixty other hired hands along dusty trails pockmarked with late-day shade, wiping sweat off their grimy faces as the wannabe celebrity camp director prattles and points to where his handlers will be supervising the camp's tried-and-true activities: arts and crafts, basketball, canoeing and kayaking, dance, drama, drawing and painting, Earth lore, fencing, guitar, hiking, horseback riding, journalism and photography, mountain climbing, pet care, pole vaulting, ranching, riflery, singing, sewing, soccer, tennis, tomahawk throwing, videography, volleyball, and zip lining.

Already exhausted, Myles and company finish their tour at the dining hall, a throwback to his school cafeteria days, with little improvement. Incandescent lights illuminate rows of extended folding tables and sky-blue walls with flecking paint ten years overdue for a fresh coat. Staff line up along the empty buffet tables in the back to rehydrate, swigging ice-cold lemonade from paper cups. They also meet Jeanie Scruggs, the camp's owner, a vivacious lady in her fifties with bright blue eyes and white curls bursting below her cowgirl hat.

"What do you think?" Jeanie asks, sorting through a box of uniforms on the counter, eyeing Myles's size. "Will a large do?"

"Yes, ma'am."

Jeanie tosses him a forest-green T-shirt with the camp's tree-hugging logo emblazoned in white, and winks. "I heard you did well in your interview. It's always nice to have a natural leader around here."

"Uh … I'm just grateful for the opportunity," Myles says. "Uh … thank you."

Jeanie smiles, and Myles takes a seat. *Last time someone called me a 'natural leader' was my first-grade teacher after I found myself in the front of the line leading my classmates out to the schoolyard during a fire drill.* Trying to avoid public scrutiny ever since, he gazes around the dining hall like a lost pet and notices the rest of the counselors present are older than he is. *Hopefully I haven't bitten off more than I can chew. Now that I got the job, I might actually have to live up to the hype.*

Geo sits on the front table, feet planted on a seat, shorts showing off his hairy blond knees. He blows a whistle, and the side conversations pause as he assigns each counselor activities that they will oversee during the camp's first session. Roles and duties are determined quickly as the many able-bodied individuals present share their impressive skills and abilities. Even José, Myles's new comrade, is given a large amount of responsibility, supporting the camp's athletic and music programs.

At last, Geo's eyes peer over his clipboard, into Myles's soul.

"How about you, newbie?" he says. "What can you offer Camp Friendly Forest, besides your charm?"

"Good question," Myles says, clearing his throat. *How long can I keep up this charade that I have anything to offer at all?* "What else do you need around here? I can do a little of everything."

The older, more experienced counselors turn away and resume their side conversations.

"Can you … throw hammers?"

"Uh … I can throw ninja stars."

"Ninja stars?" Geo says with his award-winning grin, silencing his staff-audience with his popular voice. "You hear that, folks? Myles can throw *ninja stars*." He gazes down at the freshly hired counselor. "Please, tell."

"Uh … when I was a kid, maybe ten or so, Mom let me go to the swap meet with a friend," he says. "I brought my allowance money, and I bought her a little frog statue, which she put on the kitchen windowsill. It remains there to this day."

"Uh-huh," Geo says. "Go on."

"At the swap meet, I also bought a set of ninja stars," Myles admits. "They were shiny and cool. I wanted to believe they came from a samurai stronghold in Japan, except inscribed on them were the words, 'Made in China'—"

"And?" Geo says. "What did you throw them at?"

José shakes his head and gazes down at the table, too embarrassed for his friend to listen further.

"Once, in high school, I was home sick alone while my parents were at work … there was a knock at the door," Myles says. "I was in bed and didn't answer, figuring they would go away. They didn't. The knocking was followed by tapping on the window. Still, I didn't budge. Then, I heard the living room window shatter."

It's as if the oxygen in the dining hall is sucked up at once, and silence settles in the room as Myles's co-workers hold their breath and wait for him to continue.

"Whoa," Geo says, grin melting away. "What did you do?"

Even Jeanie, sitting with her boxes of T-shirts, gazes at Myles, waiting for him to tell the rest of the story.

"I reached under my bed, opened a shoe box, and withdrew my ninja stars," Myles says. "I tip-toed toward the living room, and I found a dirty-looking guy with raggedy hair and soiled clothes trying to slither into the house through a busted window."

Myles swallows. "I don't know what came over me. I was scared to death, but I was also *pissed*, you know? I felt like crap, but the thought of running out of my house made me feel worse. None of it seemed fair, or real. I stepped in front of the guy and yelled at him to go away. I threw my five-pointed ninja star at him as hard as I could, and it bounced off his forehead. He screamed and ran."

A round of laughter.

"Now, I keep the ninja stars in a box underneath my bed at my parents' house ... just in case."

"Just in case, *what*?" Geo asks. His grin is back and looks like it's about to explode.

"Just in case there's another home invasion, and I have to use my ninja stars ... to stave off intruders."

More laughter.

Geo puts down his clipboard, and he impersonates throwing a ninja star at a home intruder, and the ninja star bouncing off the intruder's head. More laughter.

"Oh, my, I needed that," Scott says. He points at Myles. "We definitely ought to put this fella in charge of the tomahawk throwing."

More laughter.

"I second that," Richard says. "He should be telling stories, too. Might as well put him in charge of the Earth-lore thingy."

"Aye," says a third man, Matt.

During the camp tour, Myles overheard that these three vestiges of the long-disbanded British Empire acquired temporary visas that allowed them to travel to California to help staff Friendly Forest. Richard is a balding gent in a Manchester soccer jersey, Scott a New Zealander with shaggy brown hair, and Matt an Aussie in a Bora Bora hat. They met on the net, and they plan to head off together after their stint at camp to Yosemite, Shasta, and the coastal redwoods before they return to their home countries at the end of summer. Myles notices they also tend to think and act as one mind.

"… and if you're any good at kicking a ball, we'd love to have you on our football team," Scott says. He spits an ice cube into his cup. "Or what do they call it here … *soccer*?"

"Yes, soccer—but no thanks," Myles says. "I will gladly lead campers in tomahawk throwing and storytelling, but I'm not much of an athlete, nor a team player, so I'm going to have pass."

"That's funny, Myles," Geo says, continuing to hold court from his imaginary throne at the front table. "In your interview, I definitely recall you *bragging* about how much of a *team player* you are."

"Busted," José says and turns to the three foreigners. "How about I join your international team. My family is from Mexico, and we know how to play nice with others."

"Great," Scott says.

"But just so you know, soccer really isn't the sport of choice around here," José says.

"Really?" says Richard. "What is?"

"Capture the Flag," says a young woman munching on a bag of chips. She brushes the curly bangs out of her face and dramatically licks the seasoning off her fingertips. "We consider it the ultimate game."

Myles realizes that she is the one he saw coming out of the *Trading Post* when he arrived. There is a pause as the hivemind of Scott, Richard, and Matt consult each other with baffled eyebrow exchanges.

"How do *you* know Capture the Flag is an important camp tradition?" José asks. "Did you work here last summer?"

"I did," says the woman, crumpling her empty bag of chips. As she heads toward the trash bin, her large breasts jiggle beneath her tank top. "My name's Tiffany."

"Right!" José says with sudden recognition. His brown cheeks turn red. "I remember you now. My, you have … grown."

"How observant," Tiffany says, tossing the crumpled bag into a recycling bin. "Would you like a trophy, or can we give them to the campers instead?"

A round of laughter.

José returns to a topic that he is more comfortable navigating than female anatomy: sports.

"The kids love Capture the Flag, so we usually follow their lead," he explains to the expats, recovering his cool. "Have any of you ever played?"

Scott, Richard, and Matt grunt: *no.*

"You'll like it," Tiffany assures them. "It's a lot of fun."

Her friendly smile immobilizes the hivemind.

"It's settled, then," Geo says with his deal-making grin. He removes from the table a book of Native American creation myths, stacks it on top of a box filled with tomahawks, and shoves the box into Myles's arms. "Tomorrow, when the campers arrive, you'll be teaching them Earth lore and how to toss these weapons. And, of course, everything you know about *teamwork.*"

The next day, the invasion begins. Children ages eight to fourteen come from far and wide to laugh, cry, and explore a wilderness away from the confines of civilization.

José oversees a group of urban youngsters new to the great outdoors. They arrive by bus from the inner city, bringing with them minimal luggage and maximum wonder about their surroundings. He nods to Myles as one boy disembarks, hops onto a boulder, and scans the redwoods with jaw-dropping reverence.

"You see that?" José whispers. "Happy to be here, quiet for now, but watch out! I bet he'll be a terror when we get into the woods for Capture the Flag." José waves him their way. "Hey, young blood, what's your name?"

"Tony," the boy says, hopping off the boulder.

"Nice to meet you, Tony. I'm José, your counselor, and this is Myles."

"Nice to meet you, too, Mr.—"

"—Rodriguez and Harper," Myles says, "but you're welcome to call us by our first names."

"Okay ... thanks," Tony says, scrambling up another rock.

"He'll never call us by our first names," José whispers. "I'm telling you, that boy is raised *right*."

Myles turns to his own tutelage. Instead of arriving by bus, the children he supervises are delivered by luxury sedans from suburban neighborhoods across California. For these boys, Myles discovers, attending Friendly Forest is a time-honored family tradition and practically a birth right. In other words, the camp serves as a dumping ground for generations of eager mothers and fathers who are in route to exotic vacation destinations without their annoying spawn in tow. Compared to the youth José manages in *Passionate Pursuits*, the tweens in *Whispering Dreams* tend to have entitlement issues and maladaptive behaviors. As they settle into Cabin 5, Myles withdraws Supernova Cid from his duffel bag.

"I'd like to introduce you to a friend of mine," he says, holding up the doll. "I grew up as an only child, and this was my first companion." He hands Cid to the boy next to him. "Why don't you tell us something about yourself … Chris, right?"

The chubby ten-year-old nods. "Your doll feels slippery." He sniffs it. "And it smells like sour milk." His face puckers with disgust. "When's the last time you washed this thing?"

A round of laughter.

"It's made with a special rubber interior and coated with nylon," Myles says, coughing, and he nervously rattles off the doll's distinguishing stats. "It's a vintage toy from the 2020s … that would go for a lot of money … if I ever wanted to sell it … not that I ever would!" Unable to solicit envy from the campers, he changes the subject. "Why don't you tell us something interesting about yourself?"

"My parents ditched me so they could take a booze cruise to Mexico," Chris says with a shrug, handing Cid to the boy next to him. "I'm not sure what else there is worth knowing about me, except I have a dog named Dog."

Another round of laughter. Ben, the boy next to Chris, takes a whiff of Cid, confirms its foul stench with a wrinkly nose, and passes it to Miguel, who waves his hand over his nostrils and passes it to Billy, a pallid child in a corner bunk with freckles and carrot top.

"How about the rest of you?" Myles says. "What's something you'd like to share about yourselves?"

"When can I play my video games?" Billy says, dumping Cid onto the floor, withdrawing a tablet from his backpack. "I got *Psycho Therapy* for my birthday!"

"Really?" Miguel says. "So cool!"

Billy's cabin mates pounce on his tablet like wolves on a fawn. Myles enters the fray, rescuing Cid from their trampling feet. Before the boys manage to turn on the game, Myles grabs the whistle dangling from the lanyard around his neck and blows. "PHWEE-EEEEEEEEEEE!"

The piercing shriek is enough to distract the wolves from their frenzy.

"We'll get to know each other better over lunch," he says. "Put away the tablet, Billy, and wash up, everybody. It's time to eat."

By the following sunrise, it's clear that the lure of *Psycho Therapy*, the world's most popular video game, remains too great a temptation for one boy who inhabits *Whispering Dreams*.

"Come on, sleepy head, it's time for the morning meeting," Myles says, watching from the doorway as the bony body slithers inside the sleeping bag.

"I don't want to go," comes a plea from the corner bunk. "I want to stay. Play here. I wanna keep trying to get my game to work."

"You'd give up water balloon fights and roasted marshmallows for a stupid video game?"

"It isn't stupid!" Billy says, his natty head poking out of the sleeping bag. "You try making a successful global entertainment franchise!"

"No, thanks," Myles says. "I'd rather work at Camp Friendly Forest and be a role model for promising young individuals like yourself." He glances out at the amphitheater. The other campers are following directions and lining up. "I'd like to help you, Billy, I really would, but you've already broken one of the biggest camp rules by being on your device. There is no wi-fi service available, except in the *Chill Room*."

Reluctantly, Billy emerges from the sleeping bag, clasping his tablet. He wears a set of glittery velvet pajamas, popular among pre-pubescents his age. He pokes the screen of his device, but to no avail. "The signal is pretty weak."

"And it will be, until you prove you are worthy," Myles explains, arms crossed. "You can't get into the *Chill Room* unless you drag yourself out of bed and join the living long enough to earn a digital break."

"Maybe," Billy says, pondering the possibilities. "First, I need to get dressed and brush my teeth."

"What you're wearing will do," the counselor assures him. "The other kids are wearing pajamas, too. You can brush your teeth after breakfast."

"Fine," Billy says, resigned to part ways, at least for a moment, from his tablet. He lumbers out of bed, sliding his feet into his slippers, and trudges out the door.

"Good talk," Myles says, shutting off the lights.

From sunup to sundown, Mr. Harper oversees the dozen children assigned to *Whispering Dreams* while he remains half asleep, corralling them and any hopes he has for an uninterrupted slumber. The fun starts at 7 a.m. with a jarring, electronic rooster announcing on the public announcement system, "COCK-A-DOODLE DO!"

The fun doesn't stop until the closing ceremony at 7 p.m. with all children accounted for in their bunks.

It's Myles's job as counselor to protect the campers, of course—a professional Band-Aid dispenser ensuring the brood under his care wakes on time, drinks, eats, and heals all wounds, physical and psychological. To accomplish this task, he also sees himself as a standup comedian, never short on sarcasm to spur the youth on their way. Half conscious, shuffling forward, arms outstretched, chasing his dream of rest like an underappreciated zombie, the counselor crams a wedge of garlic bread between his teeth and squeezes in a trip to the bathroom to relieve his besieged bladder during sweltering days of organized chaos that keeps him teetering constantly between mirth, mania, and existential fatigue:

• "Gather around, boys and girls, and listen to this lame story about garden fairies who get into trouble for littering."

• "Washing your hands *after* you eat defeats the purpose, like wiping your butt *before* you poop."

• "Try not to dismember each other with those Tomahawks, okay?"

• "Remember, in life you're only as good as the last food sever you tipped—"

José whacks Myles's arm. "You're snoring, homie."

"Oh, sorry—"

"Look who's checking you out."

The top dogs of *Whispering Dreams* and *Passionate Pursuits* are seated on the highest row of the amphitheater overlooking a throng of exhausted staff and tireless campers. The sun's setting rays shine on the trunks of the redwoods, transforming them into brilliant columns of crimson, reflecting wheelhouses of florescent green leaves and enchanting spokes of light as the half-blind, bedazzled gatherers collect their thoughts during the day's closing ceremony.

As Ms. Scruggs approaches the stage, Myles follows José's gaze to Tiffany, sitting in the front row. The junk food queen's head is turned their way, grinning with surprisingly white teeth, despite her fondness for eating salty, sugary treats filled with food coloring.

"She's not checking *me* out, fool, she's checking *you* out," Myles says to José, eyes-half-closed. Before he returns to a state of catatonic bliss and continues his nap, he feels another whack to his arm.

"No, she isn't checking me out or you out," José says with a tinge of disappointment. "See for yourself."

Myles opens his eyes, follows José's nod back toward Geo, standing along the guard rail behind them, crotch parallel with Myles's face.

Geo waves at Tiffany; she waves back.

"I should have known," José whispers. "Dude gets all the girls, until they realize he's a creep."

"Really?"

"Every summer. You'll see."

Myles feels a firm grasp on his shoulder, and from the corner of his eye, he sees José wince from a hand that clasps his neck.

"Can you two knuckleheads keep it down, please?" Geo whispers behind their backs. "Our benevolent leader is trying to speak."

"Sure, boss," José says, gritting his teeth.

Geo lets go of them and waves at Jeanie, who blows a strand of silvery hair away from her face and gazes up at her director with a nod. Her plaid shirt is rolled to her elbows, and her thumbs rest on a golden belt buckle as she stands proud at the podium in a pair of jeans and boots.

"Now that you've had a chance to acclimate to Camp Friendly Forest," she says to the crowd of campers and counselors, raising hand to ear, "I just wanna know … are we having fun yet?"

Hoots, hollers, and howls, along with clapping hands and stomping feet, echo through the amphitheater.

"I can't hear you!" she hollers back, and the jamboree of noise continues until her hand falls from her ear back to her buckle. "That's more like it." The noise muffles into silence. "My mother and father, Bob and Betty—rest in peace—started this camp fifty years ago. It was a way for youngsters like you to come together, deepen your understanding of yourselves, and help you better connect with the world around you."

Jeanie pans the amphitheater to see if her remarks register. Seeing faces like Myles's filled with groggy tranquility, she truncates her pep talk. "So, remember, ladies and gentlemen, while you're here, be good to yourselves and to each other, and you'll have a terrific time!"

The campers and counselors re-animate with hoots, hollers, and howls. Their clapping hands and stomping feet echo into the evening sky. Jeanie waves at Geo, who steps onto the stage, guitar in hand.

"Older campers from Cabins 13 and up are welcome to stay for the evening bonfire," he says, strumming a chord. "For the rest of you, let's part ways this evening with a song, shall we?" He begins, "There was a hole."

> Campers: "There was a hole!"
> "In the middle of the ground."
> "In the middle of the ground!"
> "The prettiest hole."
> "The prettiest hole!"
> "That you ever did see."
> "That you ever did see!"
> "And the green grass grows all around all around ..."
> "And the green grass grows all around!"

As the song continues, Myles feels a sudden and unexpected sense of peace and belonging. The celebration of youth, optimism, and longing permeates his body like the sun's final rays, and despite his fatigue, the chorus of children singing tugs at his heart, dissolving his cynical façade.

Maybe this summer will be special, after all.

Chapter 3

For Myles, the unconscious world is often as frightening as the waking one. Despite a pleasant day at Friendly Forest, that night he has a disturbing dream. Lost in a sea of humanity, he roams his alma mater, Fairfax High School, confused and disoriented about his schedule. He wanders from classroom to classroom, surrounded by old, weathered, but familiar faces—peers with wispy hair clinging to balding heads, skin drooping from pale cheeks. Before him, a vast hallway lined with lockers, filled with half-animated skeletal students on the march to decomposition, resigned to their fate. Hell is to be stuck on a campus of the undead with no possibility of escape.

"Stefani?" he cries, but the words fumble from his lips, slippery and dumb like used dentures. The girl who once experimented with his heart in physics class has transformed into a geriatric without a blink of recognition, just a scowl on her face as she shuffles past him with a cane, the fault lines on her forehead marked with age and regret.

"Beat it, scrub!" she hollers, a nasty octogenarian witch.

Myles flees Stefani, and the rest of the army of undead alumni, and hides in the restroom. After struggling at the urinal with his zipper for an eternity, he succeeds at relieving himself, but it's little consolation as he stumbles to the sink and washes his hands. There, in the mirror, he beholds a ghastly vision—himself, extrapolated by perhaps a century—a wretched curmudgeon cursed to wander this ghostly campus, unsure how to matriculate.

"Be cool, stay in school!" shouts the zombie-like senior citizen grimacing at him in the mirror, teeth crumbling from decay.

Someday, that old man will be me, and only if I'm lucky.

Myles is startled awake. In the distance, the faint sound of laughter, but as he lies and listens, he only hears snores from the surrounding bunks. *Maybe it's my imagination?* Wait, there it is again. Light and rollicking, like distant thunder.

His hands reach for his phone, his feet slide into his sneakers, and after several bumps and thumps, he sneaks out of the cabin as quietly and stealthily as a failed ninja. Abandoning his post is a big no-no, but obviously others at camp already abandoned theirs, and he's curious to see who's having fun at this wicked hour.

Stepping out of *Whispering Dreams*, however, he is immobilized with fear. Friendly Forest is immersed in a depth of darkness he has never experienced, a blinding blackness that feels all-consuming, terrifying to the bone.

What is this place? None-existence? I've already graduated from high school, so it can't be hell …

Myles recalls a horror movie in which the protagonist falls into a sewer, and when her vision adjusts, she finds a throng of goblins surrounding her. He waits, breathes, as the pitch blackness of the wilderness around him takes on a form that becomes clearer, and his panic abates. Above, a half-moon shimmers through pockets of bony branches, illuminating cabins and a snaky trail. A hundred yards away—the length of a football field, maybe—he spots a dim light, the camp's health office, the only sign of woke civilization in sight.

Again, there it is, high-pitched laughter echoing through the night. His phone has no reception in this wi-fi dead zone, but it does include a handy flashlight, and he uses it to illuminate his path, warning critters of his approach. His sneakers scrape the dirt as he boldly walks toward the health office, struggling to locate his peers. As he wanders through Friendly Forest, alone and tucked in a blanket of darkness, he begins to feel more at ease. He shuts off his phone's flashlight to get his bearings. The health office is no longer in sight, but he recognizes a cluster of boulders.

He reaches a clearing. By day, this field serves as a meeting ground for counselors who prattle off names from clipboards of campers who in turn rush off to activities without further thought. After the sun sets, however, Myles realizes this open space provides visitors with a different opportunity, to stop and gaze upon the cosmos. The stretch of stars above appears to be within arm's reach. He is surprised by how much he recalls about the twinkling orbs. *Maybe a high school education isn't bad, after all.*

The vague swath of creamy light spreading across the sky is the Milky Way. It is interconnected by several constellations, a few Myles recognizes. He plops down on a patch of grass and studies the awe-inspiring span of the universe. The black silhouette of his finger traces the stars that make up Sagittarius, the stick-figure archer. There's Hercules, the hero with a narrow waist, and Libra, the only constellation to represent an inanimate object. From Myles's vantage point, Libra's triangle and two dangling strings look like a party popper—a cheap firework—not the weighing scales of justice.

This is awesome! For thousands of years, humanity has stared into space, recognized patterns in the sky, and created myths—a whole system of divination, astrology—based on those observations. Stargazing evolved into a science, astronomy, and today there is more known about how the cosmos operates than ever before. Divination, it turns out, is wishful thinking: the future is not set.

Even so, millions of people, including Myles's own mother, track their horoscope with the hope of gleaning insight into their lives. Perhaps they find it comforting to think that the stars influence them and answer burning questions—that the hand of fate guides humanity on a path toward meaning and purpose. Unfortunately, science—that same science that tells people that that their world is dying, and it's their fault—suggests that if there are any gods hiding behind the stars, there is no proof they listen.

People are masters of their fate. Today, astronomers can predict what the phase of the moon will be in one hundred years, but humanity still struggles to understand what existence means in a galaxy filled with one hundred billion planets, but only one Earth. Myles lies on his back, his gaze fixed upward until the stars blur and his consciousness fades. The same wisdom applies to himself. As much as the world may be doomed, headed for an environmental, capitalistic catastrophe, the fact is he is free. Free to think and do differently. Free to fight for a better world, a world he wants. He hopes to never wake from this peaceful slumber, but wake he does, and with overwhelming dread.

His left eye opens to find another eye peering into his.

Don't blink.

The pupil of the bear is like a black hole sucking Myles's head towards its jaws.

Don't breathe.

Musty fur, putrid saliva, Myles does not dare to flinch—or gag—as the bear sniffs his nose, and its tongue licks his lips. If Myles reacts, he could be killed. He didn't come to Friendly Forest to become a bear's meal, but to prove to his parents, and to himself, maybe, he has a life to look forward to.

Don't crack.

As the bear slobbers Myles's cheeks with spit and stink, it does so with a gentleness that does not involve its teeth. *Still, if this carnivorous creature starts to nibble on my ears or gnaw on my head, that's it! I'll smack it in the face with my phone and bolt back to* Whispering Dreams *until I'm either snug in my bunk or torn to shreds …*

Myles's T-shirt and sweatpants are poked, prodded, and ruffled as this king of the Sierras determines what it wants to do with him. Finally, the black blob lumbers past, and out of the corner of his eye, Myles spots a family of bears, their dark fur absorbing the moonlight. Together, they meander through the clearing, into the forest, away from the camp.

Myles sits upright, scrambles to his feet, and stumbles backwards until he feels safe enough to turn away from where he last saw the man-sniffing monsters and sprint toward the lonely lit bulb of civilization. He dashes around the corner of a cabin toward the health office and—SMACK! He slams into Tiffany. They flop together onto the ground.

"What are you *doing*?" she loudly whispers, tossing his legs off her stomach.

Myles rolls onto his hands and knees, eyes wandering like loose marbles. He sees the Friendly Forest van parked in the lot. Its interior is illuminated. Geo emerges from the side door, waving a bottle of wine in the air.

"Tiffany?" he calls softly. "Come on, babe, I was just kidding!"

Myles staggers to his feet and regards the young woman. Her hair is tossed, lipstick smudged. "What are *you* doing?"

"Getting away from that jerk!" she snaps, brushing the dirt off her skirt and marching toward the cabins.

Myles follows, shining the phone's flashlight on their path.

"Are you okay?"

"No."

"Want to talk about it?"

"No!"

"I was just sniffed by a bear."

"Did you throw ninja stars at it, to scare it away?"

"I tried, but it ate them."

Tiffany laughs. It occurs to Myles that it was her voice that lured him out of bed in the first place, but he would come off as a stalker if he told her that, and hasn't she already dealt with enough creeps for one evening?

Still, Myles feels compelled to be honest with her about *something*.

"I never threw my ninja stars at a home intruder."

He waits for Tiffany to respond. She keeps walking. The silence, uncomfortable, forces him to keep up with her pace.

"During the break-in, I locked myself inside my bedroom and prayed I'd be left alone as the intruder roamed around my house. As I huddled under the covers, I remember hearing the doorknob jiggle. I was so scared, I peed in my pajamas! But that was all that happened. Whoever the intruder was, he made off with my mother's jewelry and my father's watch, but I was left untouched. My ninja stars never left their shoebox."

Tiffany scowls. "Why did you lie?"

Myles tries not to trip as they walk. "Why did you go into Geo's van?"

"Looking for attention, I guess."

"Yep. Sometimes, I feel a need to pretend to be someone I'm not."

Tiffany stops. "Did you really just get sniffed by a bear, or was that a lie, too?"

"It's true, I swear," Myles says, facing her. "I had a bad dream. I couldn't sleep. So, I stepped out of the cabin to get some fresh air. I laid down under the stars … and I woke up with a big furry beast licking my lips."

"And you got away?"

"There was a whole family of them. I played dead until they wandered off into the forest, and that's when I raced back to camp … and collided into you."

"See, maybe sometimes hanging tight *is* the best move," Tiffany says. "If you confronted that intruder in your house, perhaps you wouldn't be here right now."

"I never thought of it that way," Myles says. "I just felt ashamed for being so scared."

"Nothing wrong with fear," Tiffany says. "Better to play dead than to be dead, right? The key to fighting is using your head. You gotta know when it's worth it."

As the young woman's words seep into Myles's skull, he realizes they are standing in front of her cabin, *Lovely Daze*. "Tonight, we both had a close call," she says, studying him. "Let's keep our encounters to ourselves, okay?"

Her curvy figure glows in the moonlight.

"Your secret's safe with me," Myles says, "as long as you're okay."

"I'm a survivor," Tiffany says, opening the cabin door. "I'll always be okay."

"I get you," he says. "I think. Good night."

"Good night."

Chapter 4

She waits in a booth at the back of the diner, red hoodie draped over her head, sandy-blond curls covering her face.

"A newspaper?" asks a male with a scruffy chin and headphones draped over his ears. "You're pretending to read a *newspaper*? *Really*?"

He scoots into the booth across from her before she responds, a juvenile attempt at catching her off guard.

"You can't hide behind the headlines, Alice," he says, removing his headphones, offering them to her. "Listen. Agents surround this place. They know we're here. *Together*."

Alice's eyes remain fixed on the page. He resigns himself to her indifference, hanging his headphones around his neck. After all, she supposedly knows what's coming: today, tomorrow, the day after that, a vision as accurate and inevitable as polar bears going extinct, the collapse of the housing market, and artificial intelligence changing human life forever. None of it is 'news,' at least not to 27-year-old Alice Walker, so perhaps there's another reason why she's holding up the *San Francisco Chronicle* to her face as if it were a shield.

Maybe, it is. Here at Veggie Terri Ann's in Oakland, California, where bracelets jangle on cooks flipping coconut flapjacks, and customers sift through digital horoscopes searching for answers to life's burning questions, *maybe you just want to feel like you're one of the crowd, even if we both know you're the oddest flavor of the bunch.*

"Hello, Gus," Alice says, finally, discarding the newspaper and revealing a notebook on the table between them. *The* notebook? She lifts her head long enough for her eyes to absorb his. Suddenly, he's back at the Institute, drowning in trauma. He cannot help but recall the struggle he, she, and other 'patients' endured fending off the extraterrestrial presence that infiltrated the facility and threatened to take over their minds.

What did we call that mysterious race? The Merkasy? The Marlozi? Damn ... Ah! ... The Markahzi. That's it!

How could Gus forget? But for a decade, he almost had, embroiling himself in a series of clandestine activities to earn a living and avoid the past. Now, he and Alice are adults, free to involve themselves in adult activities, so when she texted him that morning after so many years of silence, he felt obliged to respond. To meet. And yet that feeling of her eyes on his—the crushing truth of those dark, all-knowing pupils—opens a vulnerability in his gut that he can taste in his mouth, as strong as black licorice.

"You look like a fugitive on the run."

"I *am* a fugitive on the run," he says, noticing the shade of purple under her eyes. "When's the last time you slept?"

"About the last time you ate."

As if on cue, a waiter with a swirling moustache arrives, presenting Gus with a cup of coffee, breakfast burrito, and fries.

"Exactly what I was craving," he says with a wink to the waiter. "She knows me so well." Then, to Alice, "Thanks."

"Enjoy every bite," she says. "You've got a long road ahead."

The waiter's mustache twitches. "Is there anything else I can get you two? More tea, miss?"

Alice shakes her head.

"We're all set," Gus confirms, squirting ketchup on his fries. When the waiter leaves, he stuffs the burrito in his mouth. "Why the date, darling?"

"You wish," Alice says, sipping the last of her green tea. "Although, I admit, it's nice to see you again."

"I r-ew it!" Gus says, chomping on bits of egg. "You *do* r-ike me!"

"I'm not sure 'r-ike' is the right word," Alice says with a smirk. "Besides, soon, you won't like me."

Just like that, Gus's shoulders sag with the weight of the world. *She is up to something. Something big.* He finishes his bite and takes a sip of coffee. "What do you think the agents lingering outside the diner want with us? All I heard them chatting about on my scanner is a social media post—"

"They're here to observe," Alice says matter-of-factly. "They want to know what's coming."

"Who doesn't?" Gus says, rolling his eyes. "Lucky for truth, justice, and the American way—you *do* know what's coming, right?"

Alice sighs. "A challenge awaits."

"Oh, god, I hate it when you talk like that!" he snaps, tossing a fry into his mouth. "Just because you're some kind of freaky fortuneteller doesn't mean you need to *talk* like one. The world has enough problems without its savior sounding like Joan of Arc." He wipes ketchup off his lips with his napkin. "After so many years, of course you still know how to press my buttons, don't you? You know *everything*. So, let's cut to the chase, shall we? Why do you need a computer hacker, like me … to help a woman, like you … manage whatever madness you're up to?"

"I don't need a computer hacker. I need a delivery driver. One I can trust. With my life."

"Huh. What's the delivery?"

"Me."

Alice's eyes roll up to her head, and her face falls flat onto the notebook.

"What the hell?" Gus shouts, scrambling around the booth, sitting her upright. Beneath her lids, Alice's eyes oscillate back and forth.

The waiter reappears. "Oh, my!" he exclaims, staring at Alice. "What happened? Is everything ... okay?"

"Everything's ... great!" Gus insists, tucking Alice's notebook under his chin, yanking her out of the booth. The attention of the diners shifts from their horoscope readings and meals toward Gus and the comatose woman in his arms. "My friend here is just having one of her diabetic conniption fits ... I told her to lay off the sugar cubes with her green tea, but does she listen to me? Never!"

As Gus drags Alice's unconscious body out of the diner, a bystander with caterpillar eyebrows steps away from his stool, blocking their path. "Where, exactly, do you think you're taking this young lady?"

"To the hospital," Gus says. "Help me, please. Open the door!"

The bystander's caterpillar brows roll with wonder, and the waiter's mustache flickers with suspicion. After a moment of consideration, the bystander props open the front door to Veggie Terri Ann's, grabs Alice by the legs, and joins Gus in hoisting her away. "Where's your car?"

"There!" Gus says with a nod, and the notebook slips from his chin and flops onto the sidewalk. He glances down at a mix of indecipherable drawings that capture his eyes. *THAT is what's inside Alice's legendary diary of predictions? Dumb DOODLES?*

"You mean, you want me to help you load her into your *van*?" the bystander asks, gazing at the company name sprawled along the side door: *Security Breach Services, Inc.* "I mean, is this for real, man? You're not, like, some serial killer, are you?"

"If I were, would it really make sense for me to tell you?"

The bystander ponders the comment as Gus tucks Alice's unconscious head between his legs, reaches down, and picks up the notebook. Again, he lodges the notebook under his chin. "I'm an old friend of hers—I promise—not some jerk she just met on the net. Now give me a hand, will you … please?"

The bystander gazes at Gus, unconscious Alice, and the van.

"The hell I will!" he decides, finally, letting go of the woman's lower extremities. Alice's legs fall onto the sidewalk, and the bystander points at Gus. "You drugged her, didn't you? It isn't a trip to the hospital. It's … an abduction!"

The waiter watches intently from behind Veggie Terri Ann's front window. Pedestrians along the street gather and gawk at the grungy guy in a gray sweatshirt and jeans, in desperate need of a shower and shave, with a woman's head propped between his legs.

Way to go, genius, Gus thinks to himself. *This does NOT look good.*

The ends of the waiter's mustache twitch like two possessed antennae. He bangs on the window and gestures to his phone. "Enough nonsense! I'm calling the cops!"

"Excuse me, ladies and gentlemen," Gus announces to the gathering mob, "but I really don't have time to stick around and convince you that I'm not a psycho."

As Alice's head remains wedged between Gus's thighs, he wrangles the keys from his front pocket, presses a button, and the van door slides open, revealing a cabin full of dazzling electronic equipment. The bystander steps back, gazing at the instruments, his caterpillar brows working overtime with concern.

"What do you *do* to these poor women?"

Gus rolls his eyes. He places the headphones over his ears, the keys in his mouth, and he covers Alice's ears with his hands.

He bites down with his teeth, pressing a button on the keys.

WHHHHHAAAAAAAM!

An ultrasonic blast bursts from the van, ripping through the neighborhood. Veggie Terri Ann's front window shatters, the waiter cowers, car alarms ring along the street. The bystander and crowd scatter.

"It's like Grandpa always said," Gus mumbles, "if you don't have anything good to say, get out of the way."

Across the street, inside a parked sedan, a crack appears on the windshield.

"What was *that*?" says the front passenger, uncovering her ears.

"Not sure," says the driver, sitting upright. "A sonic weapon, maybe. An E.M.P., perhaps?"

"I can still hear both of you," says a voice over the radio, "so it couldn't have been an E.M.P. Your electronics work fine."

"My ears definitely do not," says the passenger, wiggling them with her fingers. "I feel like I was just slapped by a gorilla."

"Whatever it was, it worked," says the driver, bald and bearded, pointing across the street at the fleeing crowd.

"He's loading her into the van," confirms the passenger, a brunette with freckles. "Should we send in the team?"

"Are you sure it's *him*?" says the voice over the radio.

"Positive," says the passenger. "How could I forget? Involved in the Bank Holiday when he was just a teen, but he hasn't aged well. Taut and bony. Probably skips meals. Still, I never thought I'd be able to thank him myself. Enough cash flew out of the ATM machine that day for me to pay my rent for a year—"

"You're kidding, right, Agent Evans?" says the voice.

"Not at all!" says the agent, eyeing her partner. "What would you have done, sir? Just leave the money on the ground?"

There is silence for a beat, then a round of laughter.

"Let's keep that joke between us," says the voice over the radio. "No one at F.B.I. headquarters needs to know that one of our star detectives, back in the day, benefitted from the greatest cyberattack in history."

"What now?" says the driver, changing the subject.

"Follow them, Agent Moore," says the voice. "If Henrik Gustavo is involved, this might be a set up."

"Whose?"

"Hers."

"The psychic's?" asks Agent Evans as Gus starts the van. "But she's … *unconscious*."

"That's what you think," says the voice over the radio. "Remember, Alice Walker's brain works differently than ours, operating on timelines we can't see. Stay close, and don't interfere. We need to know where he's taking her."

"Copy," says the driver.

As Gus's van pulls away, the F.B.I. sedan shifts into gear.

Chapter 5

When he awakens, Myles's grogginess takes a backseat to the morning's mirth. Capture the Flag, the greatest game of Camp Friendly Forest, is set to disrupt the campers' and counselors' regularly scheduled activities. Today, Myles will not be required to regale bored children with tales about the perils of human beings destroying the Earth, nor will he be required afterward to prevent those same bored children from maiming each other with tomahawks. Instead, a ninety-minute match, scheduled after breakfast, is set to pit young against old, boys against girls, and campers against staff in a competition that demands cooperation, strategy, and courage for a team to win.

"This is your chance to show us how much you have bonded with your peers and are able to work together to undermine your opponent," says Geo, who despite his feigned seriousness with a rousing speech, teeters as he talks and has the faint glow of wine-stain shining on his lips. He points to a bulletin board posted outside the dining hall and suppresses a smirk. "Teams and rules are ready for your review. This is the most important day of your stay, Friendly Foresters! See you in half an hour on the battlefield."

As children scramble to dump their dirty dishes and exit the dining hall, Myles strolls behind the exodus with José.

"My boys are so psyched," José says, admiring the frenetic energy as *Passionate Pursuits* clusters around the bulletin board. "You'd think they're competing in the Olympics."

"You started talking about Capture the Flag the moment they arrived," Myles reminds him. "You've done a good job of hyping it up."

"True," José says. "Make sure your boys wear lots of sunblock, but no hats. They'll lose 'em in the chase. And tell 'em to bring water."

"Uh-huh."

Myles notices José watching Tiffany, who stands near the bulletin board. Arms folded, hair wrapped in a bun, she gazes off in the distance as campers shout, bark, and point at team lists and rules. Geo approaches her from behind, wraps his arms around her waist, and whispers in her ear. Tiffany flings his hands off her and storms away.

Geo catches José's stare, and Myles's body recoils as his two co-workers glare at each other.

"What did you do to her?" José hollers.

"Nothing," Geo says, sticking his hands in his pockets. "She's not as innocent as you think."

A sudden possibility of violence, palpable in the dry mountain air, makes Myles feel nauseous.

"Fine," José says. "We'll see where that attitude gets you."

José follows Tiffany toward her cabin.

"What do you say about *that*, Myles?" Geo yells, his million-dollar grin restored. "A nice day to separate the men from the boys, isn't it?"

Geo doesn't wait for Myles to respond. As the camp director slips into the crowd, Myles imagines an apex predator stalking its next prey.

Two teams—Spark Plugs and Live Wires—assemble as the sun punches holes through a canopy of forest shade, causing glistening globs of sweat to form on the foreheads of campers and counselors exposed to the penetrating rays of the high Sierra summer. Jeanie, master of ceremonies, hands a representative from each team a flag emblazoned with the auto-part insignia their group has been sworn to protect.

"Go forth, have fun, and try not to get hurt," the Friendly Forest host merrily warns her flock. "When you hear the whistle blow, the raucous begins! Don't get tagged by your opponent while you're on their turf, or you're a prisoner. First team to return their opponents' flag to their own pole wins!"

There are cheers as the Spark Plugs and Live Wires scatter to opposing sides of the creek. José scrambles to the top of a boulder, shouting over a throng of teammates clustered around the Spark Plug flag.

"The key to victory is stealth," he announces. "I'm heading into enemy territory with a group of warriors, for a sneak attack."

There are claps, fist pumps, and other signs of encouragement. José hops down from the boulder and handpicks a few select Spark Plugs to join him on his mission.

"What about us?" Matt asks, loitering by some bushes with the two other expats. "We didn't come from across an ocean just to sit on our arses and watch *you* get the glory."

"Of course," José says with a grin. "Come with me. But whatever happens, homies, *just don't get in my way.*"

The statement cracks like a midday thunderclap, and José's friendly expression contorts, revealing strain. The change in disposition does not go unnoticed by the expats.

"As long as you're running with the flag and not wiping your arse with it, there'll be no interference from us," Scott says, followed by cackles from the hivemind.

"I'm coming, too!" Tony says. The Filipino kid from *Passionate Pursuits* admires the woods only a little less than he admires his counselor.

"No, I need you to stay here and help Mr. Harper fend off the Live Wires. You're so fast, you'll chase 'em all away. Can you do that for me?"

"I guess so," Tony says stoically, shuffling toward Billy and his posse of athletically challenged participants.

Jeanie's whistle rings, and José disappears with his infiltration force. A plume of smoke rises into a blood-hazy sun. Somewhere, a wildfire is ruining someone's day. The fires, they all know, will blaze from that moment in June until the rains come in November, all the while threatening the stability of California. As for the trees surrounding the Spark Plugs, they remain windless, eerily still and quiet, as the camp's make-believe conflict over the forest ensues.

Myles, Tony, and the rest of *Whispering Dreams* set up an ambush behind a cluster of bushes on the Spark Plugs' side of the creek, where they squat, wait, and swat gnats, trying to be patient long enough to not blow their cover.

"How long is this going to take?" Billy demands, slumped on a stump, fanning his face with his hand. "I'm hot."

His remark sets off a chain of whining.

"Me, too!" says another camper.

"Yeah, this game sucks!"

"I want to go to the *Chill Room*, where I can cool off and play a *real* game," Billy moans.

Tony, perched on a nearby branch, shushes them. "Live Wires are coming!"

Myles peeks through the foliage, and sure enough, Tiffany and several comrades from *Lovely Daze* assess the rocks that span across the rushing water.

"What do you want me to do?"

"Stay here," Myles tells Tony. "I will surprise them when they cross, then you tag as many as you can as we force them back to their side of the creek."

Tony gives Myles the thumbs up. Myles taps Billy on the shoulder, and he and his fellow party poopers grudgingly follow along the trail to defend their flag.

The Spark Plugs take position behind a boulder and listen as the Live Wires splish-splash across the creek. A girl slips, falls, and plunges into the current, followed by laughter. Myles peeks around the bend, and Tony signals back to him, counting them off with his fingers: *one, two, three, four, five* ...

Like innocent fawns, they dart past the tree in which Tony lurks.

Myles counts to himself. *One-one thousand, two-one thousand, three-one thousand* ...

He leaps onto the path, arms raised, growling like a wild beast straight out of Earth lore. A line of approaching feminine faces screams. As the Live Wires flee back toward the creek, Tony leaps down from his hiding place in the tree, and together Myles and he scramble to tag the stragglers.

Tiffany detours away from her team, drawing the two males with her. While the rest of the Live Wires manage to return safely to their territory, Myles and Tony surround the counselor around a redwood tree. The little guy tags her.

"You gave me a workout ... I desperately needed ... to clear my head," she says, panting as she slaps Tony high five. "Nice job, dude."

Together Myles and Tony escort their prisoner along the creek. On the other side, the safe Live Wires make funny faces at them.

"That was a great play," Myles says, catching his breath. "You made us chase you, so you could save your cabin."

"Like the great Jeanie Scruggs once said, Capture the Flag is all about strategy and teamwork."

"For some," Myles acknowledges, pointing toward camp, as Billy and the other conscientious objectors stroll past the Spark Plug flag on their way to the *Chill Room*. "For others, it's about not breaking a sweat."

"They'll grow up, eventually," Tiffany says with a wave. "One day they'll realize that girls don't want to sit around and watch boys play with their joysticks all day."

"Huh?" Tony says.

Myles erupts with laughter, but his gaiety is drowned out by adrenaline-fueled shouting in the distance.

"What's that, Mr. Harper?"

"Let's find out."

Myles leads Tony across the flowing water, over a cluster of fallen trees, and to the top of a small hill. Near the Live Wires' flag, they spot the expats, arms spread and holding back a crowd of campers as Geo and José square off in the center of the human circle. Myles cuts through the throng and finds himself standing between the camp director and his counselor buddy, two hawks ready to swoop in on each other and strike.

"I'm a lover, not a fighter," Geo insists, fists raised. "Come on, man, you don't want to do this!"

"Is that what you call yourself, a *lover*?" José snickers. "I got another word for you, *pendejo*. I'm gonna teach you to keep your hands to yourself!"

José leaps into the air. Geo catches him mid-kick, slams him onto the ground, and pommels him on a one-way trip to unconsciousness.

"Keep my hands to myself, huh?" Geo shouts with psychotic glee, knuckle-punching José on the nose, mouth, and forehead. "Like this? Maybe you … ought to be less concerned … with women who don't like you … and find one who does!" he shouts between blows. "I didn't do anything to her that she didn't have coming her way!"

As the beating unfolds, the expats and campers stare in disbelief. Not Myles, however. Something inside his soul snaps. One moment, he watches on the sidelines as José is mauled by Geo, and the next, he's a star running back ploughing over the alpha jerk.

"What the hell, Myles?" Geo yells, hands sheltering his face as the younger counselor pummels him with his fists. "I got no beef with you!"

"Too bad!" cuts Tiffany's shrill voice through the sweltering summer air, "cuz I've got a beef with *all* of you!"

She stares at her coworkers with infinite disgust.

And just like that, the violence ceases. There is a tug around Myles's shoulders, and he's hoisted to his feet by the expats. Geo rolls to a sitting position, a gash on his cheek. José, slowest to recover, props himself upright, face a bloody mess. All of them turn to find Tiffany in tears, standing at the edge of the circle, lips flush with outrage.

"I didn't ask ... for any of this!" she screams, eyes flashing between Geo, José, and Myles. "What's *wrong* with you?"

Silence.

"And you?" she says to Myles, desperate for an answer. "Why did *you* get involved? Why didn't you ... *hang tight?*"

Myles, at a loss for words, appears as confused as Tiffany, who does not wait for him to respond. She stomps off, leaving the young men with their own thoughts.

In shame and silence, they march back to camp.

Chapter 6

"This is Radio RQR with your favorite tunes!" shouts a fast-talking deejay from the van's dashboard. "Bet you're wondering if I need to pee, because I sound like I'm in a hurry, but maybe I'm no human at all, just an A.I.-algorithm playing tricks on you! The secret is mine, for now, but here's one I can't hold in any longer: 'Heartbreak Street' by Lani Waits will take you down a road of love and loss, leaving you breathless and searching life's lonely streets for answers …"

Gus hangs a left onto the interstate on-ramp.

"Is it say-f to come out now?" says the voice of a boy with a thick Russian accent. Glancing in the rearview mirror, Gus watches the bobblehead unfold from a tucked position behind Alice's shoes. The bot meets Gus's gaze with his beady eyes, combed-over hair, and wrinkly synthetic skin. "No more sonic boom-boom?"

"All clear, Mr. Pootin," Gus assures the mini menace—larger than a doll, but smaller than a toddler—as the van merges onto the freeway. "That blast you heard was just a deterrent, to help us flee the diner. No more sonic boom-boom."

"Dat's good, cuz it hurt my ears!" says the bobblehead, plopping onto Alice's stomach, elbows resting on her breasts, gazing down into her closed eyes and tranquil face. His nostrils flare, imitating the woman's as she inhales and exhales in her unconscious state. The bot pries open her mouth, examining her teeth. "Is she your det?"

"Is that what you call a knocked-out woman traveling in the back of a van?" Gus asks. "A *date*? In this country, we call that a felony."

"Then, what do you call a crime?"

"You misunderstand," Gus says, swerving the vehicle into the fast lane. "It's not a date, or a crime. I helped her get out of a jam."

"I see," Mr. Pootin says. "You removed her from a jar of jelly."

The bot in his black suit and drab tie stands on Alice's stomach, kneading it with the soles of his dress shoes, assessing her red hoodie and blue jeans. "She dresses okay for a North American. I think I vill like her, but she can use my fash-on advice."

Mr. Pootin steps onto the cabin floorboard, leaps, and lands in the front-passenger seat next to Gus. He turns up the volume on the radio, and his over-sized head bobs back and forth to the last lines of "Heartbreak Street."

"I love deez love songs!" the bot exclaims, clasping tiny hands together with nostalgic glee. "This von reminds me of Gretta. Vee vorked together at satellite factory in Odessa. Sometimes, vee sneaked out to local hot spring and indulged in night of dan-sing, vodka, and caviar!"

"You two didn't actually drink vodka, or eat caviar, did you?"

"Of course, vee did!" Mr. Pootin declares, twiddling his thumbs. "Vee made so many sveet touchy-feely memories under da stars!"

"I doubt your experience with Gretta was that … intimate," Gus says, glancing sideways at the bot. "You realize you're a zero-hearted, battery-operated batch of aluminum, don't you? A knock-off of the twenty-first century's most despised dictator? In other words, you *can't* drink vodka or eat caviar, because you lack the organs to digest—"

"How dare you deny my hu-man-ity, Henrik Gustavo!" Mr. Pootin shouts. The bobblehead lunges onto Gus's shoulder, causing the van to swerve. Knives slide out from the bot's fingernails, ready to strike—

"Back off, bro!" Gus shouts, flinging the bobblehead off his shoulder into the back of the van.

Mr. Pootin lands in a ball on Alice's stomach, starts to sniffle. "You hurt my feelings. No fair."

"You could have gotten us killed!" Gus yells, steadying the van. "Never try to … slice my throat … while I'm driving!"

"It depends on how nice you are to me," the bobblehead says with a mischievous grin.

Gus takes a deep breath and measures his words.

"Look, Mr. Pootin," he says, glancing at the bot in the rearview mirror. "I'm not sure how I can make our relationship any clearer to you. A Russian oligarch gave me a gift for hacking into a computer system and retrieving him valuable information. At that time, I thought his present to me—you— were a practical joke, and during the months that followed, with you faithfully nagging me by my side, I've become convinced of it. The oligarch promised me that you'd be useful. Instead, you are now the bane of my existence."

"Vhat brain?" Mr. Pootin says, frantically looking around the van. "Between you and me, I see no brains here …"

"*Bane,*" Gus reiterates. "It means … never mind."

As traffic slows, Gus brakes as his mind races for the right words to convey his frustration with the bot … without getting himself killed. "I guess what I'm trying to say is—what's your problem, dude? Why the psychopathic tendencies? Do you feel unloved? Neglected? Did Gretta dump you?"

"No," Mr. Pootin says, head downcast, shoulders slumped. "Sorry, I just pro-grammed dis vay." The bobblehead scrambles up to the workstation, sits on a stool, and gazes at his reflection in the computer screen. He straightens his tiny tie and perks up. "Cut me some slack, vill you? Admit it, no von dresses as vell as me!"

"True," Gus says, glancing back at the bot with an empty smile. *And more truth: How many near-death encounters have I had with this homicidal bobblehead? How much longer can I keep the peace?*

Mr. Pootin pulls the edge of the workstation and spins himself on the stool. "Vee!" he shouts, rotating round and round. "Vee!"

As the bot spins, his pupils rattle like loose marbles.

Crazy Russian.

"So, how long haf you known da voman?"

"Alice?"

"*Da!*" Mr. Pootin shouts, clasping the edge of the workstation and ceasing to spin. His marble eyes settle into their sockets as he focuses down on her unconscious body. "Of course, silly. Your det."

"She's not my *date!*" Gus snaps, glancing at Mr. Pootin's reflection as the bot sits in the back of the van. "That woman is no damsel in distress, and I'm no prince! Get those archaic notions out of your head. It's 2036!"

"And yet, you know her?" the bobblehead inquires with genuine curiosity. Or as genuine as he gets.

"It's a long story," Gus says, gripping the steering wheel as the van accelerates past a lane of stopped vehicles. "We are two lab rats on the run from the same government."

"In-ter-es-ting," Mr. Pootin says, rubbing his chin. He withdraws his teeth from his mouth and places them on the workstation. The teeth flap and announce, "Please, sir, share da juicy details!"

A deluge of angst bursts from an internal damn as memories of the Institute flood Gus's head. *Maybe it would be good to talk about that period in my life, even if it is to a miniature dictator. Even better, maybe* me *talking will keep* his *mouth shut for a while.*

"Fine," Gus decides, and he swerves the van toward the freeway exit. "You opened up your emotional processors and told me about Gretta, I guess I can return the favor and tell you about Alice."

"Yay!" Mr. Pootin's teeth shout as he shoves them back into his mouth. He hops off the stool and lands on Alice's stomach, stroking her hair and whispering. "Hear dat, my luf? Henrik Gustavo is going to tell a story."

Los Angeles, with twelve-million residents, seems as good a place as any to hide from law enforcement. Heading south in that direction, Gus grants the bobblehead's wish and takes a detour off the interstate.

While the van seems to have distanced itself from Oakland and its agents, a whiff of smoke alerts Gus to the fact that he and Alice remain within range of danger. Wheeling around a bend, he spots firetrucks and helicopters scrambling like ants around an immense blaze, a hellish conflagration along the Coastal Ranges to the west that threatens to engulf the Central Valley's golden fields of dead grass.

A Liberator—a mech likely used to fight the Oil Wars, now retrofitted to battle Western wildfires—thunders down from the sky and lands next to the blaze. Pinkish flame-retardant spews from its mouth onto the inferno. The effort makes little difference, however, and a sense of impending doom ticks off Gus's anxiety. The unimaginable climate crisis that scientists predicted last century has become widespread and unmanageable, a war pitting humanity against nature. And humanity is losing.

Gus parks the van at a rest stop, but on Mr. Pootin's insistence, he lets the vehicle idle. A heat-resistant film applied to the windows helps to keep the interior cool, but with midday temperatures soaring at one-hundred-and-twenty degrees, the protective layer is not enough. The bot reminds driver to keep the air-conditioning running so that 'sensitive' electronic equipment onboard is not damaged.

Withdrawing a handkerchief from a suit pocket, Mr. Pootin wipes his brow, pretending to dabble sweat off his forehead. He settles with legs crisscrossed on Alice's stomach. Gus's eyes shift from the pensive gaze of the bobblehead in the rearview mirror to the scene ahead through the windshield: a lone water fountain, restrooms, vending machines, and pockets of struggling agriculture—mostly agave—surrounded by fields of kindling ready to ignite. How long until flames reach the rest stop?

Back when California was nicknamed the 'Golden' State, Gus is certain it had little to do with parched farmland inflicted by a decade of drought—soil so withered it no longer feeds the world, as it once had, and now provides only enough food to sustain a regional population. He withdraws his phone from his pocket and scrolls until he finds what he is looking for. He reaches back and holds up the screen to the bobblehead. "Recognize this?"

Mr. Pootin glances up at the ten-year-old Bestagram post:

BIG QUAKE MOURNING – 9:32 P.D.T. 8.25.26 – MILLIONS SUFFER THE RISE

"No," Mr. Pootin says. "Should I?"

"Those are the words that made the woman you are sitting on famous," Gus says, glancing at Alice, human floor mat. "She not only predicted the Big One, but also the political upheaval that followed."

"Let me see dat!" Mr. Pootin hollers. He scrambles toward Gus's hand, snatches the phone, and resumes his position on top of the unconscious woman. He gazes at the screen. "Is it code, or some-sing?"

"More like a message," Gus says as the bot admires Alice's profile. "A metaphor—and a call to action, so to speak. Very few people heard, or heeded, Alice's prediction before the Coastal Earthquake, but after the destruction ensued, news of her clairvoyant consciousness spread, and she became a social-media sensation. In time, the quake triggered the kind of political shifts that led to California and other regions seeking further independence from the United States—and Alice led the way, opening the minds of millions of people to a future they could embrace. However, she was also an orphan, so no one knew where to find her outside of cyberspace. She was finally apprehended by detectives at a Venice coffee shop in December 2026, several months after the quake."

Mr. Pootin pats Alice's nose. "If she sees future, vhy she not drink coffee some-space else and a-void *politsya*?"

"A good question, Mr. Pootin, and to my point: Alice *led* the detectives to her because she *wanted* to get caught."

"Huh?"

"She wanted to confront a foe not even the government could defeat— a foe not of this world. Being captured was the only way for her to do so."

Slamming doors. A husband, wife, and twins disembark from an SUV like a brood of dehydrated ducks, shuffling toward the water fountain, taking turns drinking and filling bottles. Gus points out the windshield, beyond the ashen clouds of dust and gloom overlooking the Central Valley, to the faint shadows of the Sierras to the east. "Alice was taken to the Institute, a secret installation far from here, where her psychic powers proved to not only be legitimate, but something that the scientists studying her were unable to explain in any logical or reasonable way."

"Wow," Mr. Pootin says, eyes on the phone. "How do you know?"

"I was there," Gus says, once again gazing at the bot. "Some believe Alice's mind operates outside the boundaries of known physics. Others believe the mysteries of her mind simply haven't been solved yet." He notices the notebook he tossed next to Alice when he loaded her into the van. He turns back and points, "Hand me that, please."

Mr. Pootin flings the notebook to Gus, who faces forward after he catches it. He thumbs through the pages, pondering the meaningless doodles and designs—that is, until the right person comes along at the right time, and bam! The answer to some critical question beyond the typical reach of space-time is revealed—a drawing or phrase that helps the beholder resolve a dilemma—or so the legend goes.

"Is this nonsense, or a miracle?" Gus asks, raising the open notebook, pointing at the scribbles. "What do *you* see?"

Mr. Pootin could care less, more interested in scrolling on Gus's phone than gleaning cosmic insights. Gus flips to the last page, grabs a pen from the glovebox, and writes in bold caps, 'TRUST GUS.' He turns back with a smirk, showing the entry to the bobblehead. "See? There's even a mysterious message in here about *me*."

The bot glances up, rolls his eyes, and continues scrolling. Despite his shortcomings, Gus realizes, Mr. Pootin is no fool.

"Did you know Droop Capone, da famous rapper, refers to Ms. Valker as 'Lady Pro-Fit'?"

"You mean, Lady *Prophet*?" Gus says, closing the notebook. "We're not talking about a woman selling a line of athletic wear, pal. Alice has a very unusual skill set." With no response from the bobblehead, Gus crams the notebook between the driver seat and center console. *Better keep Alice's diary close to me until Mr. Pootin is ready to take the world's future a little more seriously ...*

"As for me, the skills that led to my stay at the Institute can be explained by more conventional means," Gus says, gazing out the windshield at dying fields ripe for incineration. "Growing up, they called me The Wizard. I was a computer nerd—too smart for my own good, perhaps—but it was only after I blew a full ride to M.I.T. and joined a gang of revolutionaries determined to save society that I started to make headlines." He pauses to check if Mr. Pootin is paying attention. "Perhaps you've heard of my exploits, stored inside your memory bank? Surely, the

Russians didn't hand you over to me without providing you background on your guardian?"

"You are *not* my guardian!" Mr. Pootin shouts, gazing up from Gus's phone, pupils burning like fiery coals. Knives slide out of the bot's knuckles. "Or do I need to teach you a-nudder lesson about playing nice, Henrik Gustavo?"

"Nooooo!" Gus insists, raising his hands up to the rearview mirror in surrender. He turns back toward the bot with renewed humility. "My bad, Mr. Pootin. *Sir*. We are business associates. Allies. Equals. Everything's … cool."

The knives retreat, and the reddish gleam in the bobblehead's eyes fade. The bot continues to review Alice-related news. "Did you know dare is a hula-hoop cheer-letting squad called Da Little Red Riding Hoods? Day appear at football games and car shows and pay homage to Lady Pro-Fit … in red hood-eez!" The bobblehead glances down at Alice. "Like the von she vears now."

"They're not the only ones who believe Alice is special," Gus says. "A lot of people follow her online."

"Indeed!" the bobblehead exclaims. "Seventy-five million fall-overs … and counting! Ms. Valker is more popular den Nancy McMuggins, da first celebrity actroid!"

"The actroid's Oscar-winning performance impersonating a grieving mother in that dumb drama is old news," Gus says, trying his best to keep his jealousy of Alice's fame in check. "Anyway, my comrades and I hacked into the nation's financial system on President's Day in 2026. During our notorious 'Bank Holiday,' we forced A.T.M.'s across the country to dump cash onto their customers. We transferred billions from the accounts of the wealthiest Americans to the poorest. We were real renegades! True supporters of the people! We also made some powerful enemies.

Eventually, the government proved itself competent enough to catch me for my crimes."

Gus gazes at the family of dehydrated human ducks at the fountain as they guzzle and replenish their water supply. "Eventually, the youth imprisoned with me at the Institute managed to escape, and I have avoided government detection since—until today."

Staring at the wildfire raging in the distance, Gus hopes California's climate mitigation plan, created to locally manage global warming, proves in coming years to be more than a public-sector failure. Otherwise, the once lush and fertile Central Valley will transform permanently into a charred wasteland as barren as the moon.

"Even though my arrest—in a rare instance—occurred because I was outsmarted by authorities, Alice set herself up to be captured because she wanted to confront the elusive monster she knew waited at the Institute. She was the only Earthling, you see, capable of saving the planet from such a menace."

Mr. Pootin glances up from phone, meets Gus's gaze.

"Mon-ster? Men-ace?"

The bot rolls off Alice and hops back into the front passenger seat. "Did your encounter today with Lady Pro-Fit have some-sing to do vith dis?" Mr. Pootin asks, flashing Gus's phone in his face. On it, Gus sees Alice's Bestagram page has been updated with her first post since the 2026 Coastal Earthquake:

INVASION – 2:35 P.D.T. 6.28.36 – MIND YOUR ESCAPE

"What?" Gus shouts, grabbing his phone. "*Mind your escape.* How did I miss *this* message?"

Mr. Pootin shrugs. "Perhaps you need to pay less atten-shon to da past, more atten-shon to present?"

"Shush!" the hacker snaps. Alice's latest missive to the world posted three hours ago, just before he met her at Veggie Terri Ann's, and it is spreading faster than the wildfire in their midst: ten million likes. "Are the Russians preparing to drop paratroopers on the West Coast, or something?"

"How should I know?" Mr. Pootin says, raising his hands. "I haf no beef vith your country." With a sly grin, the bot points out the windshield. "But remember, my friend, joost because *you* are paranoid, does not mean *day* are not after you."

A glance outside the van reveals a surveillance drone hovering one-hundred feet above. A sedan parks three spaces to the right. Inside, a male driver and female passenger, in suits and shades, turn toward Gus.

"I'm pretty sure those two followed us from the diner."

Mr. Pootin cackles like a villain in an old spy movie. "No escaping da government for you, Henrik Gustavo!"

Chapter 7

"You think he's on to us, Tom?" asks Agent Evans as they watch Henrik Gustavo lock eyes with them across cars in the rest stop parking lot.

"He knows we're following him," says Agent Moore, "and he's probably just figuring out why. He's not as smart as they portray in the media."

"You sound jealous of him."

"Listen, Rudy," Tom says. "They *literally* caught him with his pants down on a toilet seat in a hotel room in Mexico back in 2026. He fled there following his infamous cyberattack, but he had no idea the government was onto him. An agent down there, a buddy of mine, said the journalist who broke the news story about his arrest decided to play nice, because Gus was a minor at the time, and so she reported that 'The Wizard' was found asleep in bed during the raid. Less embarrassing, I guess, than getting caught while taking a crap. Her version of the story, however inaccurate, is the one that stuck in the press."

"At least we got him."

"*Had* him," corrects the voice over the radio. "Henrik Gustavo and other gifted individuals who studied at the Institute were more resourceful than we anticipated. But we'll have him again, soon, along with Alice, the main asset, of course."

A boy-like creature with a patch of thin hair, creased brows, and two beady eyes pokes his head up from the passenger window.

"Who's the twerp peeking out at us?" Rudy asks. "Gus's kid brother?"

"Ha!" says the voice over the radio. "Not a blood relative, and that's a good thing, since Gus probably wants to kill it—"

"It?"

"A bobblehead," the voice says. "We believe that a Russian business tycoon recently presented Gustavo with the artificially intelligent doll as a gift for successfully completing a hacking assignment. A tiny physical replica of the old tyrant, Vladimir Putin, the bot offers the fugitive occasional logistical support, but its main function is to serve as a surveillance system for the Kremlin, providing regular updates about Gustavo's actions and whereabouts. From what I understand, the bot is also very annoying. The Russians hope their mole will lead them to Alice."

"Looks like it has," Rudy notes. "And that beats trying to keep up with Gus on the road. Such an erratic driver! Didn't notice us following him, either, until now. How many times did he almost swerve into us?"

"Too many to count," Tom agrees, mesmerized by the exploding popularity of Alice's Bestagram post. Eleven-million likes, 12-million likes … "If we don't nab them soon, somebody else will. A rabid fan, or worse …"

Tom flashes his phone at his partner:

INVASION – 2:35 P.D.T. 6.28.36 – MIND YOUR ESCAPE

"… the invaders will!"

"Very funny," Rudy says. "But Tom's got a point, boss. Isn't it time for us to bring them in?"

"Soon," says the voice over the radio. "We've set up a roadblock on the interstate. If the trouble starts as soon as Alice predicts, we believe our checkpoint will be the safest way to capture them."

The triumphant Geo and defeated José hobble forth from the forest, each carrying their own sack of worry, leading a trail of dazed campers and counselors struggling to make sense of their scrap.

"Will Geo and José get fired?" Tony whispers.

"Probably," Myles says. "Me, too, I'm sure. Fist fights are generally not tolerated at a workplace."

"Stinks."

"It does," Myles says. "I was just starting to enjoy this job."

Myles marches ahead, side by side with José.

"How are you holding up?"

"I'd be better if you hadn't jumped in."

"You're welcome."

José glances at Myles with a swollen eye—the size and shape of an avocado growing out of his forehead. "I told everyone to stay out of my way, but instead you had to get into trouble ... and make me look weak."

"Better than Geo making you look dead."

Behind them, the expats chuckle.

"Still talking smack, or what?" Geo asks, glancing back at the duo.

"Nah, homie," José says. "Just telling the truth."

Geo stops, José and Myles stop, and so does the rest of the caravan. The camp director—at least his title for now—turns and approaches José, pointing at his chest. "What's it gonna take for you to keep your frick'n mouth shut?" he asks, balling fingers into a fist, showing off the flecks of blood still covering his knuckles. "At this point, *homie*, I have nothing to lose."

The expats shake their heads in collective dismay.

"Enough!" Scott shouts, clasping Geo's shoulder. "You're setting a bad example for the kids."

Geo refuses to lower his fist, however, and Myles feels his whole being pivot. Instead of his usual fear—fear of this world, fear of all its terrible problems—a well of outrage swells to the surface. *None of this is right.*

"What's the *deal* with *you*?" he asks, unleashing a verbal barrage onto his supervisor. "I thought you were the cool dude around here—practically a celebrity—but now? First, there's whatever you did to Tiffany, then this tough-guy act? You're a creep, you know that? It's bad enough this camp hired a fool like me, but to think, they put *you* in charge—"

"Everything was fine until José started to mess in my business," Geo says matter-of-factly, staring down his nemesis.

"Still won't admit you crossed a line, will you?" José responds, baring his teeth. "Homie, no matter how banged up I might be, I'll never back down from you!"

Gus reverses the van, and it squeals out of the parking space.

"Vhy are vee leaf-ing?" asks Mr. Pootin, thumbing the two agents in the parked sedan. "Don't you vant to karate-chop da spooks?"

"Nah," Gus says. "The only thing I'm good at chopping is broccoli. Besides, haven't you heard the expression, 'Choose your battles?'"

Mr. Pootin buckles himself into the front passenger seat. "In Russia, vee say, 'A bad peace is better den a good fight.' Same i-dea." The bot holds up Gus's phone. "But never mind vhat *vee* say, Henrik Gustavo. You should read da comments about Alice's post! Da sheeple believe Ms. Valker has predicted da end of da vorld!"

Gus glances at the dashboard clock: *2:34 p.m.*

"In that case, we're a minute away from the apocalypse," he says, punching the accelerator and rocketing the van onto the freeway. He proceeds until the van's speed matches the outside temperature—one-hundred-and-twenty—weaving through cars and trucks, grateful that driving so fast and recklessly with a hydrogen-combustion engine, even if illegal and dangerous, is a climate-neutral activity.

If only the global economy were designed with as much skill and sophistication as the company car for Security Breach Services, Inc. Gazing in the rearview mirror, Gus's grin grows as the distance between himself and his pursuers increases until, finally, the sedan is so far behind, it is out of sight.

"We lost 'em."

Mr. Pootin's neck extends, and his head surveys the scene, not behind, but ahead of them. A line of brake lights signals an upcoming traffic stop. The bot corrects driver. "You mean, day found us."

As Gus focuses forward, his smile morphs into a frown. Half a mile ahead, a cluster of black SUVs and police cars form a checkpoint-barricade. He checks the time on the dashboard and tightens his grip on the steering wheel: *2:35 p.m.*

A sound, like a sonic boom, rattles the forest. The eyes of Myles, José, Geo, and the rest of the counselors and campers turn upward. A gust of wind rushes through the redwoods, and a murder of crows burst from their perches in the branches above, the black scavengers cawing noisily as they scatter into the sky.

"Earthquake?" asks one of the expats.

A wave of shimmering light, a kaleidoscope of color, immerses everything around them in a spectacle of beauty and warmth. It's unlike anything Myles has ever seen, like showering under a rainbow.

"Whoa," someone mutters.

The gust of wind dies, the birds are gone, and the consciousness-expanding light fades as quickly as it arrived. The impact of passing color, however, is something that Myles can only begin to imagine. *Something extraordinary is happening.*

A veil of indescribable light unfurls from the sky. The wall of unfolding color spreads across Southern California, blinding Gus, who slams the van's brakes. He covers his eyes with his hands and peeks through the cracks in his fingers at the spectacle that unfurls before him. The radiant barrier consumes all within its reach—swallowing a flock of seagulls suspended in the air, devouring parched fields, and burning hillsides. Even a vehicle charging station, twinkling like an aluminum oasis, is absorbed by the strange psychedelic phenomenon. Mesmerizing, blinding, beautiful. For a moment, Gus has no desire but to surrender himself to the approaching mirage, but the bobblehead jars him to his senses. The bot flips backwards off the front passenger seat and buries his face in Alice's bosom.

"Da in-vay-shon!" shouts Mr. Pootin with a muffled voice, unwilling to look up from Alice's breasts.

Of course! It's as if Gus's brain is struck by lightning, reanimating his paralyzed body. He swerves left, accelerates, and drives over the dirt shoulder, through a median of bushes, across oncoming traffic—except there is none, because vehicles traveling from the south are devoured by light.

"Da pretty colors are eat-sing every-ting!" Mr. Pootin cries, glancing up in time to witness the roadblock vanish. The van bounces over gravel and shrubs, riding alongside the oncoming hallucinatory wave.

"Goodbye, Henrik Gustavo!" yells the bot from the back of the vehicle. Instead of being enshrouded in the dazzling veil, the van hits a jutting rock that sends it sailing.

Gus feels the kind of freedom he hasn't experienced since he was a boy being tossed into the air by his grandfather. When the van returns to the Earth, his head zooms in on the steering wheel faster than the speed of thought. Instead of stars, all Gus sees is black.

Tony, patting his body, gazing at his hands, says, "When I arrived at camp, these redwoods seemed so magical, but they aren't *really* magical, are they?"

A round of laughter.

"No," Myles says, clasping the boy's shoulder. "There are no pots of gold waiting at the end of the rainbow. At least for us."

More laughter.

"Then, what just happened, Mr. Harper? What *was* that?"

"Beats me. But I want to find out."

As José takes a head count, Myles notices a crowd forming outside the *Chill Room*, the only building for miles around with wi-fi access. He points that direction, "Maybe we can get answers there."

Any interest in chauvinist politics, score settling, and toxic masculinity related to Geo and José's fist fight takes a backseat to the campers' and counselors' fascination with the inexplicable phenomenon they just witnessed. Myles and the small mob of foreign nationals and North American natives, Geo and José, friend and foe alike, scramble to the only location in sight that offers a glimpse into the outside world. Everyone, it seems, wants to know more about the mysterious wave of light that passed through them.

Joining the throng inside, Myles finds Tiffany and others spellbound. Curtains are drawn and volumes run high on the monitors arranged side by side along a row of tables. The *Chill Room*, once a place for the device-afflicted to escape the natural world and enjoy a respite in virtual reality, now resembles a military command center. There is a peculiar, effervescent haze surrounding the flickering screens, residue from the anomaly of light. Tuned to different channels, radio stations, and web sites, the images and sounds projecting from the monitors show bits, clips, and commentary about a developing story.

At 2:35 p.m., a mile-long alien ship appeared from a wormhole that materialized outside Earth's atmosphere and discharged the massive freighter, which hurtled across the sky and crashed into the Pacific. Video footage taken from surfers congregating on a hill at a beach near Marine Corps Base Camp Pendleton, north of San Diego, shows vestiges of a tsunami wiping out a portion of the Interstate 5 Freeway, displacing cars, trucks, and dragging onto shore piles of seaweed, fish, and trash. A jarring scene follows consisting of blaring horns, mobilizing troops, and soldiers arresting the blond trespassers in wet suits as fighter jets scramble through the clouds above toward the wrecked spaceship jutting out from the ocean.

Meanwhile, the real threat arrives. At first, the black heads protruding from the waves resemble otters and sea lions—marine life frequently spotted offshore. Then, the first of the four-legged creatures beaches. It's the size of a grizzly bear, but leaner, with a horned cranium, a cluster of reddish eyes, and a devilish grin that reveals rows of jagged teeth. The beast shakes its dark fur dry, strides onto sand, and points its grotesque snout upward, sniffing the air. A Marine, who had been holding her position, machine gun trembling in hand, turns to flee. When she does, the monster leaps into the air, pounces on her, and tears her to pieces.

And just like that, America is at war with aliens.

More images follow. Drone footage shows wave after wave of hundreds, thousands of predators from outer space scrambling onto Southern California's coast, terrorizing beach towns, devouring fleeing pedestrians and stranded motorists.

"Reminds me of those World War II docs they sometimes play at night," José whispers, words barely escaping his lips.

"The Normandy invasion," Myles agrees, eyes shifting from screen to screen. "But in this case, the 'D' in 'D-Day' stands for the destruction of our species."

On one computer, in the corner of the *Chill Room*, a broadcaster with a pompadour displays a social media post made earlier in the day by Alice Walker. Known as 'Lady Prophet' among her followers, Alice is said to have predicted the 2026 Coastal Earthquake. After escaping government custody, the broadcaster explains, she has lived a life of anonymity, until an update appeared on her Bestagram profile hours before hostilities ensued with the aliens:

INVASION – 2:35 P.D.T. 6.28.36 – MIND YOUR ESCAPE

As Myles absorbs news of the catastrophe, the psychic's message is like a neon sign flashing at his soul.

Mind your escape. How? What does she mean?

"They're in the neighborhood!" a dogwalker from Huntington Beach screams into a news camera. He splashes around in knee-deep water as a poodle, retriever, and terrier bark, yelp, and practically strangle themselves trying to pull free from his leash. Too late. In an explosion of blood and limbs, man and canines are overrun by the cosmic carnivores. One of the monsters rips the head off the dogwalker, tosses it up in the air with its teeth, and swallows the head whole. The beast turns toward the camera with its crimson gaze.

More screams, and the media crew goes offline.

Scientists already have a name. They call them *Kiaskis* because a burst of light in space coinciding with the arrival of the invaders suggests they originate from the Kiaski Nebula, near the Libra constellation.

"We have an idea where they come from," says a professor from the University of California Irvine, near ground zero, during a phone interview. "Unfortunately, we have no idea why they are here."

Commotion in the background, and he, too, goes offline.

"I know why they're here!" Billy yells in an upbeat tone out of tune with the devastating circumstances. "It's just like *Psycho Therapy*! They want to turn us into dog chow and make a zillion space pups!"

The proposition seems absurd, but the evidence is clear. From one disturbing image to the next, the *Kiaskis'* appetite for human flesh seems endless. Even so, only Billy and his dopey friends dare to snicker in amusement at the prospect that the end of the world might mimic its most popular video game.

"This trip to camp is turning out to be less of a dream," Tony whispers, "and more of a nightmare."

"I want to go home!" cries a girl, turning toward Tiffany, who embraces her.

"Me, too!" cries a boy, collapsing into their arms. "This isn't funny!"

The ray of light that passed, Myles thinks, *the odd glow of electronic devices, too much is happening too fast.* Jeanie sidesteps through the stunned crowd and manually turns off every monitor.

"Hey, we were watching that!" Billy protests.

"We have seen enough," says the owner of Camp Friendly Forest. The rosiness has drained from her cheeks, and her light-hearted twang is no more. Her voice is somber and precise. "I realize many of you are scared. I am, too, but we are together. Safe. You will have an opportunity to speak with your parents. For now, I am going to ask that you refrain from watching the news. I will work with staff to arrange times for each of you to connect with your loved ones. In the meantime, the *Chill Room* is off limits. Free time until dinner. We could use a breath of fresh air."

Chapter 8

Agents Moore and Evans gaze at the cascade of brilliant light that has descended upon the Interstate 5 Freeway. Their co-professionals in law enforcement—along with their imposing SUVs and police cars—have bled into the wave of luminescence and disappeared.

"Boss, our team has been swallowed … by a gigantic rainbow," Agent Moore mutters, struggling to describe the scene.

"Confirm, please," says the voice over the radio. "You have no visual contact with the roadblock?"

"Affirmative," says Agent Evans. "Our team—and all vehicular traffic in the path of the light— is gone."

"In the chatter," says the voice, "I'm hearing reports of a ship that crashed off the coast near San Diego, causing an atmospheric anomaly, a blanket of brilliant colors that covers Southern California. Agents, what's the status of this light you see now?"

"It appears to have stabilized, sir," Agent Moore says. He cranes his neck to verify the size. "Do we still have surveillance on the van?"

"Affirmative," says the voice. "The drone is online and tracking. Sending you the coordinates."

The radio display on the dashboard projects a holographic grid of the surrounding topography. The agents identify the stationary van, a pink bleep appearing in a field southeast of the freeway.

"We have a digital I.D.," Agent Evans says. "Looks like they've stopped. A half mile off the interstate. We'll take a closer look."

"Proceed with caution," warns the voice. "If Alice predicted this scenario, that means she predicted your involvement as well. You could be heading into a trap."

"Copy, boss," Agent Moore says. The sedan veers off the freeway, into the brush, and closes in on the drone's signal. As the vehicle rumbles along the glimmering wall, the rays of light cut through the smoke and haze of the Central Valley, revealing a silhouette of the Sierras to the east. Plowing over dead grass and dry shrubs, the two agents hear a loud thump in the back of the sedan.

"Did you leave something in the trunk, Tom?" Agent Evans asks, gazing at the shimmering light outside the passenger-side window. "A dead body, perhaps?"

"The spare tire must have gotten loose," Tom says, sedan zooming toward suspects. "We'll check it out after we pick up our computer nerd, sleepy psychic, and mouthy robot."

"Some days, I think we'd have been better off going into comedy, not law enforcement," Rudy says.

"Me, too."

Shifting in his seat, confused and disoriented, Gus gazes past the dashboard, and the situation becomes clear. The front end of the van is smashed into a gulley. No sign of Mr. Pootin in the rearview mirror, and the back door is ajar. Alice's body lies sideways, crunched in the fetal position under the workstation. It's as if she has taken cover from an earthquake, but there's been no earthquake, not today, only a stroke of bad luck while driving that put the van out of commission.

Unbuckling his seat belt, Gus clambers toward the back of the vehicle. He checks on the psychic. Her eyes remain closed, and her chest rises and falls. She remains alive but blissfully detached from the trials and tribulations of the living, or so the hacker assumes, but who knows where her mind is?

Crawling out of the busted backdoor, he sees the bobblehead standing on a boulder, peering up at the wall of light. Amazed to find the bot silent, for once, Gus does nothing to disturb its peace—or his own.

"Vhat *is* it, Henrik Gustavo?" the bot asks.

Looping rays swirl within a kaleidoscopic hurricane an arm's throw away. Florescent streaks of pink, orange, yellow, and purple, a collage of a million sunrises and sunsets, smeared onto a three-dimensional canvas that reaches from the ground to the stratosphere. The shimmering face is unlike anything this side of existence. That which has been enveloped by the phenomenon is no longer visible, but what does *that* mean? What happened to Southern California? What's happening beyond the veil?

"I have no idea," Gus responds. The questions are many, the answers are few, but eyeing the drone that is spying on them from one-hundred feet in the air, he realizes he at least may be able to ascertain the scope of the mystery. Returning to the van, he reaches over Alice's unconscious body and grabs a tablet from his workstation. He meanders through the open field until he finds a signal used by the drone and tunes the tablet to the same frequency. Within a minute, he gains access to the drone's central processor, assumes control over its mainframe, and begins to manipulate the machine's hardware.

"Wave goodbye to Big Brother," Gus says, gazing up at the drone's camera.

"I haf no siblings," the bot laments, watching Gus engage with the tablet. "I am only child."

Gus ignores the remark as he re-routes the drone's course to better assess the size and scale of the shimmering wall. Rising higher and higher into the atmosphere, like a kid's balloon set loose into the sky, the aerial surveyor attains an altitude of nearly five-thousand feet before it ascends no more, reaches its limit, and wavers in place.

From that height, the drone proceeds with an infrared scan of the multicolored monolith. No signals, besides light waves, reflect off the brilliant cyclone. The barrier's dimensions, more so than its properties, appear to be quantifiable. A slight bend in the camera's optical view suggests there is a curvature to the anomaly, and Gus sets his computer's algorithms to calculate its size and shape. He routes the information into a quanta data storage field for future analysis, and just in time. The limits of gravity, air pressure, and other factors related to the drone's poor design run their course and force the flimsy machine's rotor to fail. The drone spins into a freefall toward Earth. While Gus hates to lose hardware, even third-rate government junk, the camera captures precious images and measurements before the machine descends into the rainbow sheer of the extraterrestrial barrier and vanishes.

Again, the question:

"Vhat is it, *really*, Henrik Gustavo?" Mr. Pootin asks, his attention on the wall of light.

"A boundary, I think," Gus concludes, "but I don't know what this boundary separates us from, or why."

"Some help you are," says the bobblehead, wagging an admonishing finger at Gus. "I could learn more from Alice's notebook ..."

"Very funny."

A sedan approaches from the west.

"It looks like the cavalry has arrived," Gus says with more sarcasm than relief. He tucks the tablet under his arm. "At least the Feds will give us a lift out of here."

Mr. Pootin hops up and down on the boulder, waving enthusiastically at the oncoming vehicle. "Yippie!" he hollers. "Meb-be day can explain dis light—unlike some genius I know."

Returning from Capture the Flag, an odd mix of hot and bothered campers, unstructured down time, and world-changing news create the perfect conditions for *Whispering Dreams* to ignite with speculation.

"If aliens have come to Earth, they're probably here to help us," Chris says, shouting his opinion from a top bunk across the cabin to Tyler, listening from a bottom one. "Otherwise, why would they bother? They can travel across the stars. We are just starting to colonize Mars. It makes sense they would be friendly. The media must be lying, like my dad always says ..."

Meanwhile, Ben, James, and Miguel find a way to cool off with a water fight. They take turns filling up cups in the bathroom sink, dashing in and out of the cabin, dumping the precious resource onto each other. Before Myles manages to admonish them for wasting water, he's drawn into the discussion.

"Maybe they'll help us produce more food, because Earth's population keeps growing, and so many people are going hungry," Tyler says. "Wouldn't it be cool if they taught us how to make *snacks* that are actually *nutritious*? Like, Mom always wants me to lay off the sugar, right? But maybe the aliens will show us how to bake cakes high in protein, or how to make licorice that won't rot your teeth!"

Myles's eyes toggle back and forth between bunks as he struggles to find the right words to reorient these young and impressionable minds to the harsh reality of humanity's first contact with extraterrestrials ...

"Maybe they'll teach us how to make snack bars that have the same vitamins as broccoli but taste awesome, like gummy bears," Chris says, "and we'll never have to eat real vegetables again!"

"Maybe they'll teach us how to teleport across the universe, like they have, and settle new worlds, like they do," Tyler says, "or teach us how to time travel."

"Give me a break!" Billy shouts over them. "You think the aliens are here to be our friends? I was in the *Chill Room* and *saw* the news. They're tearing us apart, dudes."

Ali, Frank, and Sam, huddled in the corner, glance up from a card game.

"Is it true?" Ali asks.

Ben zips into the cabin, heading for the sink. Myles blocks the bathroom door, preventing him from escaping, and wrangles his pursuers, James and Miguel, corralling the three boys together.

"Game over, fellas," he announces. "Take a few deep breaths and stay inside for a sec, because I want to talk to all of you."

Ben, James, and Miguel breathe slowly, measuredly, following their counselor's lead as Myles approaches the center of the cabin.

"Sometimes, the truth is scary," he says. "It appears that these aliens crash landed, and, no, they're not friendly. In fact, they are causing a lot of destruction right now."

"See?" Billy says.

"I don't believe it," Chris says.

"Me neither," Tyler says.

"Sounds about right," Ali says.

Geo enters. His blond streaks glisten from a recent shower, and the gash on his face is covered with a band aid. The dread on his face, Myles realizes, probably has nothing to do with work-related disciplinary action.

"It's your turn to talk to your families," Geo announces. "Gentlemen, if you have anything important to say to your parents, now is the time."

News of the *Kiaski* invasion spreads. By the time the campers in *Whispering Dreams* are situated in front of the monitors in the *Chill Room*, the notion of carnivorous conquerors from outer space seems to be normalizing.

A burst of light, a spiraling kaleidoscope, fills the computer screen for a beat and dissipates immediately as Myles's living room comes into view. His mother and stepfather are seated at the coffee table, gazing at him.

With her lips red and face powdered, Myles's mother looks more done-up than usual. Such an act, however, doesn't fool son. Tangled hair and swelling around her left lip suggest that she was more ruffled during a recent trip to the grocery store than she cares to admit.

"There are soldiers directing traffic in the streets and tanks lining major boulevards," she says, rattling off the grim realities of L.A.'s mobilization against the *Kiaski* threat. "Our trip to Organic Foods was calm and orderly, all things considered. Sure, the shelves were a little bare, and it's true that the lines were a little long, but there wasn't too much pushing or shoving. I swear. Your father and I got out fine."

Mom smiles. There are remnants of blood strewn on her teeth, and Myles sees how the lipstick she wears covers a bruise on her lip. "Martial Law has been declared, so I think your father and I are going to enjoy a date night at home, share a bottle of wine, snuggle on the couch, and catch up on our shows."

Mom blows Myles a kiss and holds back tears as gunfire, explosions, and screams ring in the distance. Al's face replaces hers on camera. The patch of hair that has clung to his head throughout Myles's adolescence is combed over nicely, and the button shirt he wears makes it seem like he is on his way to work, not Armageddon. However, his bloodshot eyes reveal the truth.

"Some kids graduate, and they head off to California's universities or attend community college," he says with unwavering duty. "Good choices. Others go wait tables at Outer Chowder Steakhouse or work from home handling customer complaints for Starlite Herbs or some multi-level marketing racket …"

Al's snicker sounds like he's choking. He continues to describe the post-high school trajectories of Myles's classmates. "A few go into the trades, and fewer still make mistakes and end up in prison." Al smiles at his stepson unapologetically. "But not my Myles. Nope! He graduates from high school … and heads to summer camp!" His cackle is followed by a cough. Tears stream from his eyes.

"And it's all for the best," he says, the sound of his voice competing with a car crash. Behind him, the living room window shatters, and the front door bursts open. Mom's cries become desperate pleas. "You're safe, son, far from this madness. I am so proud of the boy you were, and the man this life will help you to become. Stay strong. Always be good to yourself and others. Remember who loves you."

There's a growl.

"Most of all, Myles," his stepfather says, revealing an ax in his hands, "… if you ever encounter a *Kiaski* … kick its ass!"

He turns, swings.

Blood.

Teeth.

Black.

Chapter 9

This heat.

Gus could fry an egg on Mr. Pootin's shiny metal crown. He is not sure he'd want to, however, since eating it would probably give him lead poisoning. Gus tears off his sweatshirt and wraps it around his head, soaking up his perspiration. Better than dripping dust-smeared sweat that stings his eyes and itches his face.

"Two agents in da sedan, five-hundred yards and clo-sing, with bio readings in da trunk," summarizes the bot in rapid-fire succession. "I urge you to take evasive action, Henrik Gustavo. I haf a bad feeling—"

"You don't have 'feelings,' remember?"

As soon as Gus says it, he regrets it. Mr. Pootin's jaw dislocates from head and drops toward the ground in an exaggerated expression of disbelief. Suspended in the air, the mouth dangles freely.

Gus, disturbed and fascinated, manages to state the obvious. "That's … cringy."

"You vant to vaste more time dis-cussing da scope of my sen-she-ant programming?" Mr. Pootin demands, mouth expanding so wide Gus spots plastic tonsils within.

"No," Gus realizes with a sigh. "I just want you to work with me, not against me. Now more than ever. We need to stay focused and learn what is happening inside that … spectacle."

Mr. Pootin's jaw returns to its proper position as his arms extend around Gus' knees, and the bot buries his face in the man's thighs. "Thank you, Henrik Gustavo! No more Cold Var! From now on, you and I shall be B-F-F's!"

"Let's not get carried away," says the hacker, extricating himself from the bot's embrace. "We have work to do."

The sedan, followed by a cloud of dust, grinds to a halt. The agents exit. The taller of the two, a bald male with a silvery beard, looks more like a retired rocker than a government goon. He flashes his badge.

"Greetings, sir … and little sir," he says, glancing from Gus down to Mr. Pootin. He thumbs the anomaly of light. "Wild weather we're having, huh?"

His partner, a woman with a head of curly black hair in a beige business suit, looks like she could lead a band of her own. She stands with arms folded, assessing Mr. Pootin with her gaze. A third person emerges from the trunk. He has slicked back hair, wearing shades, in a track suit and sneakers, as if he were abducted while jogging. Mr. Pootin and Gus watch, spellbound and speechless, as the man casually strolls from behind the agents with a briefcase in one hand and a revolver in the other—

BAM!

BAM!

The government goons flop to the ground.

"*Dacha Putina!*" shouts the shooter.

Gus pumps his scrawny arms as fast as he can, fleeing the homicidal jogger. He hears the man re-load as Gus nears a ridge, almost free …

BAM!

A shot to his left calf.

Feels like a bee sting. Gus whimpers, limps, persists.

BAM!

Another shot, to his right shoulder.

Gus falls. Clasping dirt with hands, he manages to push himself off the ground and roll like a log onto his back. In the distance, Mr. Pootin appears paralyzed mid-stride with knives drawn, shut down by the assassin's verbal command before he could defend Gus from the murderous aggressor.

The assassin looms over Gus, a silhouette of cold, calculating violence surrounded by a halo of psychedelic light.

THUMP!

For a moment, Gus stares cross-eyed at the feathered end of a dart that dangles from his forehead.

Ouch. My brain hurts.

The sleep that follows is a sweet, merciful darkness.

Sitting in the *Chill Room*, the black monitor in front of Myles feels like a portal into his broken soul. Through the glare of the ceiling's incandescent lights, he sees an image of himself reflecting off the empty screen. The legal adult needs a shave and trim, with stubbles growing wildly out of chin, and his flat top starting to resemble a black mushroom growing out of his head.

However, it's not his failed fashion sense that irks the grungy counselor. It's his vacant stare at the young man in the monitor. Tears begin to fall from his face like shards of shattered glass.

Nor is he the only one at Camp Friendly Forest who's inner being has been cracked by the apocalypse. The responses to the assault on Los Angeles—the staggering loss of family and friends—causes a maddening chorus of shock, disbelief, and grief. Myles tries his best to ignore the deluge of sadness.

Stepping outside of the *Chill Room*, he takes a breath of fresh air. Well, not exactly fresh. The musky smell of fiery embers fills his nostrils and penetrates his skull, a jarring reminder that the *Kiaski* invasion is not the only disaster crippling humanity. Wildfires spurred by decades of drought, precipitated by climate change, prematurely put the sun to rest behind a curtain of poisonous clouds that beat the sky a sick purple.

"My parents are dead."

José, leaning against a redwood tree, vomits. His head turns sideways, bile dribbling from his lips.

"Mine, too," he says, wiping his mouth.

"I can't believe … this … this … is happening," Myles stammers, head low and hands on his knees, trying to prevent José's nausea from becoming contagious. "They were … were … so … so … good to me."

"The best," José says, stepping away from the tree, lost in his own memories. His banged-up face from the fight is now a legacy of a former life. He lifts the cross draped around his neck, presses it to his swollen lips. "The gunfire … the chaos … those ugly-ass alien rottweilers. *Dios mio*."

A girl with braces, in a camp T-shirt and flowered leggings, dashes out from the *Chill Room*, spinning in circles. "We were a team!" she shouts up toward the heavens. Her palms face upward, fingers curled as if she's carrying a heavy load of laundry. "We laughed and enjoyed doing everything together! Even chores! How could you *leave* me, Mom?"

Her attention returns to Earth and the two young men standing next to her. As Myles and José approach her, the girl's hands turn over in surrender, and the basket of imaginary laundry is dumped onto the ground. She flees into the forest, a trail of tears marking her suffering.

We each grieve in our own way, Myles realizes. *Mind your escape*.

The hot, wrenching ache Rudy feels in her gut is unlike any physical sensation she has known. *Not even my period cramps come close to this pain.* Then again, it's the first time in her career as a detective that she's been shot.

Wish I was dead, she thinks to herself. *Isn't that sick? A continued opportunity at life and I'm not sure I want it. Too much hassle.* She laughs, despite the agony it adds to her torso. She rolls onto her back, pressing stomach with hand as the setting sun breaks through a line of low-hanging clouds of ash and smoke. *California, once paradise, now a tainted land with air so foul from overdevelopment, climate change, and chronic wildfires that breathing is only a little better for a person's health than the alternative …*

But breathe Rudy does, and despite her gunshot wound, surprisingly well. She checks the status of her stomach with her fingers. A bullet is lodged and married to her intestines, it appears, but so far, blood loss is limited. Instead of a river of red running down her fingers, there is only a stream.

"Tom?" she whimpers.

She can't stand, but she can crawl, and she does so on her hands and knees through dirt, thorns, and punishing heat. Mixing the red on her palms with the brown on the ground, it's as if she's preparing a palette, her life's final masterpiece.

When she reaches her partner, he is lying face-down on a crushed sagebrush transformed into a crimson casket. She sits upright on her knees, and with all of her might rolls him over, stunned by his pale, puffy cheeks, and unflinching gaze.

"Lucky you," she says, wiping tears with her crusty hands. "At least you're no longer assigned to this lousy case. We really should have gone into comedy, my friend."

She falls to the side, rolls, and returns to all fours, scouring the immediate field around her like a half-dead search dog. The sedan is gone, but the van is not. She channels her remaining chi on the busted back door of *Security Breach Services, Inc.* At an intimidating fifty feet away, she inches forward to determine the status and whereabouts of Alice Walker.

Her final work as a detective is almost complete.

Musty motel room. Rays of light feather through cracked blinds.

Ouch.

Bright.

Brain … still hurts.

"Putin's Palace!" shouts the shooter, still in shades and track suit, seated in an armchair across from Gus. Perched on a nightstand to Gus's left, Mr. Pootin thaws from his fixed battle stance and springs back to life.

"Hi-yah!" the bot shouts, lunging toward the homicidal jogger with a flying high kick. Instead of succeeding with his attack, the bot falls from the table, flat onto the floor, caught by a mesh net that envelops him. Mr. Pootin whines and pounds his hands and feet against the stained carpet.

Interesting pattern: 'Dacha Putina,' which the assailant shouted in Russian and forced Mr. Pootin to deactivate in the field—has the opposite effect when spoken in English. 'Putin's Palace' activates the machine.

The homicidal jogger cracks a smile. "I just want you to work with me, not against me," he says to the pouting bobblehead, quoting a previous conversation Gus had with the bot. "Now more than ever."

Mr. Pootin, a gift FROM the Russians, must also be a gift TO the Russians, recording and relaying my conversations, acting as their spy. Great idea letting this bobblehead into my life! I'm starting to suspect my grandfather was right about me. High I.Q.? Maybe. Common sense? Not so much …

"Don't listen to him, Henrik Gustavo!" shouts Mr. Pootin, his limbs webbed together by the metallic threads, his arms and legs flapping on the floor in a pointless tantrum. "I'm getting us out of dis mess!"

"Please, no," Gus says, annoyed. "You've done too much already."

The bobblehead's knives expand from his knuckles, and he attempts to slice through the mesh.

"*Akva diskoteka!*" commands the killer marathoner. The knives withdraw, and the bot is declawed.

For now. The phrase provides Gus with an important clue. 'Putin's Palace'—sometimes referred to with sarcasm as 'Putin's Country Cottage'—is the world's largest home, a sprawling complex the hacker learned about one night while watching a documentary. The site, as Gus recalls, is set on nearly two-hundred acres off the Russian coast of the Black Sea. Reported to be worth over two billion, the mansion offers a variety of amenities, including amphitheater, arboretum, bridge, church, dessert shop, gas station, greenhouse, helipad, music lounge, reading room, and Turkish baths. Perhaps the most intriguing feature of the site is the *'akva discoteka'*—an undefined area, supposedly part swimming pool and part night club—where depraved parties take place.

It seems whoever coded Mr. Pootin had a sense of humor. Not only are the bot's features *restricted* using Russian commands and *freed* using the same commands in English, but the commands themselves are based on the namesake dictator's over-priced, over-sized, over-indulgent retreat. For a person with Gus's coding expertise, he is fascinated by such a game, already thinking how he can take advantage of the bot's operational parameters.

Mr. Pootin rolls over, lying face up on the floor. He gazes up at Gus, lying in a bed on his back next to Alice, the non-dating couple. Gus turns away from the bot to check on the status of his female friend, confirming with the rise and fall of her chest she is breathing. They, too, are enmeshed in a net, movements restricted by the tenacious tinsel. Not that Alice is going anywhere. Will she ever awaken? *Any 'prediction' that could untangle us from this debacle would be helpful …*

The assailant opens the briefcase, a laptop, and begins to type.

"How did you manage," Gus mutters, "to hitchhike in the detectives' trunk … without them knowing?"

The psychopathic long-distance runner removes his shades and regards Gus with eyes as dark and menacing as bullet holes. He presses a button on the keyboard. "You're not the only one with a few techy tricks," says the man's voice, except scrambled by the laptop to sound feminine, high-pitched, and sensuous. He presses the keyboard again, and this time he sounds unfiltered, masculine, natural. "I pretended to be their boss. I laid in the back of that trunk, giving them orders through an augmented voice on my computer."

"So ... what happened to the detectives' boss?"

"What do you think?" the assassin says. Gus swallows. "If you tell people what they want to hear, Henrik, in the voice they expect to hear it, you'd be surprised what you can get away with."

Still mired in the mesh, Mr. Pootin laboriously clambers up the bed and squats on the pillow next to Gus's head.

"Where are you taking us?" Gus asks.

"Russia," the assassin says, continuing to type.

"Is that who you work for, the Russians?"

Staring into his laptop, he replies, "Not always. I am what you call a 'free agent.'"

"By 'free agent' we usually mean someone looking to sign with a football team, not a mercenary for hire."

"Oh," he says, glancing up from his laptop. "Is that a problem for people, my profession?"

There it is. A slight accent. Not Russian. Turkish? If so, he's the first redheaded Turk Gus has ever seen.

"It depends on who you talk to," Gus says as Mr. Pootin leans over him. Gus's view is no longer of the popcorn ceiling above. Instead, it is consumed by the countenance of an infamous autocrat examining him. "People, for example, usually have a problem with mine. They say I'm selfish and destructive. A public nuisance. My parents disowned me years ago because of my hacking. My grandfather is the only person in the world who would still love me if he knew what I do for a living ... but he's dead."

Gus notices the killer's eyes suddenly target Gus's mouth, so Gus gets to the point. "What do *you* value?"

"Nothing," the free agent says.

"Do you enjoy killing people?"

"I don't mind it."

"Well, then, it sounds like you've chosen the right career."

The bot, never ceasing to annoy his guardian, pulls back the metal threads along his arms, as if rolling up his sleeves, making his hands as taut as possible. He proceeds to play with Gus's ears. The hacker turns his head and blows on the bot's fingers, trying to shoo him away. "Whose side are you on, again?"

The bobblehead retracts his fingers like a scolded schoolboy.

"I understand why the Russians want Alice," Gus says, glancing at his comatose accomplice. "Even unconscious, she manages to cause trouble. But, why me?"

The assassin lifts his head from his laptop. "The oligarchs have been watching you, Henrik," he says. "They think your talents are being ... underutilized. With the right guidance, they believe you could become a powerful weapon. So, you are being conscripted into Russia's cyberwarfare department."

"Huh?" Gus asks in disbelief. "You mean, you're not going to *kill* me?" He raises his head, despite its throbbing, to get a better read on his captor. "Instead, you're turning me into some kind of cyber slave?"

"Not slave. *Employee*."

"I'd rather remain a free agent!" Gus growls, trying to wiggle out of his confining cocoon. "The hell with all of this international intrigue!"

"Take a deep breath, Henrik Gustavo," says Mr. Pootin, caressing his forehead. "Dare is no need to resist. You are trap-t."

Gus blows the bot away from his face. "Buzz off, traitor!"

The bobblehead recoils. Still, air rushing from Gus's lungs leaves him huffing, puffing, and following the bot's advice. *There is no point in resisting. Yet.*

"Dat's better," says Mr. Pootin. As the hacker's breathing stabilizes, again he reaches out to caress—

"Nooooo!" Gus hollers, biting the bobblehead's hand through the mesh. The bot retreats to his side of the pillow. "Keep your creepy little fingers off me!"

Gus rests his head on the pillow, gazing at the popcorn ceiling, gathering his thoughts. "Who will train me in the ways of Russian cyberwarfare?"

"Me," says the assassin. "Your tech skills are the finest in the world—you know that—so after a brief probation proving your loyalty to your new employer, you'll be put in charge of a division, manipulating governments and markets. My job will be to support your growth in the art of stealth and deceit. You have room for improvement."

"I see," Gus says, his gaze again level with the assassin's. "And if I refuse?"

"I turn you into avocado toast."

Chapter 10

The next time Rudy regains consciousness, she is lying on her back, legs hanging from the van's busted back door, eyes gazing past the extraterrestrial light to a setting sun burrowing beneath a burning horizon. The wounded woman touches her stomach, a puddle of blood. She's amazed she awoke, but her energy is fading. Fast. If she's going to make any headway in the Walker case, it must be soon. Dying time looms.

Her eyes roll around the van. No sign of Alice. She and her entourage were likely abducted by that murderous perpetrator. His shades and track suit may have been part of a disguise, but his slick red hair looked one-hundred percent natural. And familiar. Where had the detective seen him before? On the F.B.I.'s Wanted List, probably.

Rudy musters the strength to clamber through the cabin, blood dripping from her gut. She collapses in the front passenger seat. Glancing up at the rearview mirror, the image she sees of herself is hideous. Cheeks a purple shade of death, the draining of her life's essential fluid leaving her lips pale blue. She feels as if she just tried to scale Mount Everest without an oxygen mask, and now she's an inch away from oblivion.

She lounges on the seat lethargically, ruffling stoically through the glovebox like a small-time burglar, testing the fine line, in her mind, that's always separated thievery from detective work. Fighting off dizziness and an overwhelming desire to sleep, she reaches into her suit pocket, calling her boss to provide him with an update. No answer. Figures. All of that jabber on the fancy two-way radio, but it's too much for him to pick up an old-fashioned cell phone. She rests her mobile on the center console, trembling. The inevitability of her demise, and the idea of its permanence, deepens the chill in her bones. As the sun descends west, wrapping up another scorching day, the Central Valley heat remains brutal. The gauge on the dashboard indicates an outside temperature still hovering above one-hundred degrees, but Rudy shivers violently from that which she feels and fears most.

The end for the F.B.I. agent may be in reach, but she knows the end of the world need not be. Tucked between the center console and the driver seat is a notebook, and her eyes widen from a rush of adrenaline and a renewed sense of purpose. Could it be *the* notebook, containing the legendary predictions of 'Lady Prophet?' Retrieving the journal is like discovering a favorite toy under a Christmas tree … stumbling on a four-leaf clover in a field … or finding a much-needed healing potion in a fantasy video game. Truly, an unexpected surprise.

At least, that's how Rudy imagines her discovery. The untitled composition book has a glossy black cover, worn and frayed around the edges. Contained within the warped pages are designs and doodles—scribbles that appear to be no more artistic, deliberate, or meaningful than what a toddler might muster with a permanent marker unleashed on a page.

Rudy bristles with frustration. If *this* is what she has sacrificed her life for, her life has been an abysmal disappointment. If she were a burglar, not a detective, she at least could have traded stolen art the world admired and died rich.

The F.B.I. agent chuckles, flipping through the tea-stained sheets of the notebook. No matter how long she stares—the ideas, images, and symbols flash before her eyes and disappear before she really acknowledges what she's seen—lost forever in the dreamlike chasms of her mind. Reading the notebook, she decides, is like cramming for an important exam created by a brilliant professor whose lectures will always remain elusive for most and never truly meant to be understood.

This seems to be the case, anyway, until Rudy turns to one of the last entries. Through a barrage of fleeting flowers, tombstones, constellations, and amusement park rides, an image emerges from the notebook that imbeds itself into the wounded woman's awareness:

12345678910

The three-dimensional numbers appear as blinking multi-colored digits that remind Rudy of twinkling holiday lights. Each number springs from the notebook and into her brain, proving to be the world's wildest pop-up book, digits that act as portals to a particular stage of the detective's life.

Within the first digit, Rudy sees a silent movie of herself as a bean swimming in the bright, beating cosmos of her mother's womb. Within the second digit, Rudy sees herself as a newborn child, held close to her mother's bosom as her creator, nurturer, and protector gazes down at her with doting eyes. As Rudy's attention continues to shift, she sees herself as (3) a toddler happily eating peanut butter from a jar with her fingers, and (4) a child riding a bike for the first time. Eventually, Rudy sees herself as she is now, (7) gazing in a notebook in sweltering summer heat, contemplating her life on the brink of death.

The numbers and life-like movies they show, however, do not end with those touching memories. Rudy skips to the last number (10) and is struck by an overwhelming sense of fulfillment and peace. She sees herself as an old, wrinkled woman lying in bed surrounded by an old, wrinkled, husband and two grown children. They are the loved ones she has yet to meet. Alone in the van, she gasps. "I have a whole life ahead of me."

How? The idea feels like a dream, and maybe it is. Maybe this is her brain's final farce, bathing her in dopamine as she perishes, deluding her into believing in her last moments she might persist. Still, if it is a dream, it's one she hopes continues, because the truth is, she loves the idea that the future is not fixed. Maybe life sometimes does defy its own rules, even the inevitably of its end, and there is reason to hope when even hope seems lost. This radical notion of unjustified faith causes a crack in the detective's dying ego that releases a torrent of tears. Suddenly, Rudy's heart is lifted, and she feels a serenity and peace with the world that she probably hasn't, she realizes, since she was that bean flapping around in the primordial soup of her mother's womb.

If she *is* to live, however, she had better figure out a way to do so quickly, because her consciousness can't hold this fantasy much longer. Are there more to these digits than portals to her own mind. If so, what else might the digits represent? How can they help change her current course? Rudy glances around the dashboard of the van, looking for answers. Her eyes fall on her phone, and she counts the digits on the last number she dialed. The numbers in the notebook are as long as the inputs necessary to make a standard long-distance phone call.

Hmmm. Rudy's boss may not have answered when she rang, but maybe if she tries the number provided in Alice's notebook, someone will. Rudy picks up her phone and dials 1-(234)-567-8910.

Before the first ring is complete, a man answers. "Who are you, and what is your relationship with Alice Walker?"

"This is ... Rudy Evans ... with the Federal Bureau of Investigation, and I found this number in her little black book."

"What's Alice's status?"

"Abducted. She was under surveillance, then ..."

Rudy trails off, struggling in her seat to remain focused.

"What's *your* status?"

"Dying."

"What did you see in the notebook?"

"My life. Flashing before my eyes."

"A little cliché. Anything else?"

"For me, that was plenty," Rudy says. In an effort to be diligent, however, even in the face of her own destruction, she reaches for the notebook and fumbles again through its pages. "Oh, there is something else ... something odd ... on the very last page, legible and in bold caps, 'TRUST GUS.'"

"Interesting," the man says. "I'll make a note. My name is Ray Salvatore. I am a commander with the North American Intergovernmental Task Force Security Division."

"The ... huh?" Rudy asks.

"The N-A-I ... it's not important," the commander says. "Satellite information indicates you are calling from an F.B.I.-issued mobile device southeast of the Interstate 5 Freeway at Giffen Cantua Ranch at Latitude 36.474674224853516 and Longitude -120.39237976074219 in the Central Valley of the Republic of California. That means you are less than fifty feet north of the alien anomaly that manifested at 2:35 p.m. Pacific Daylight Time today, Saturday, June 28, 2036. Is this information correct?"

"I tried calling my boss, but—"

"I regret to inform you that your boss, F.B.I. Special Agent-in-Charge Jay Schneider, was found dead eight hours ago in his home."

"That's impossible! I just spoke to him over the radio!"

"The individual who impersonated your boss is likely the same person who abducted Alice Walker. Do you have any indication where she may be?"

"Negative," Rudy says, sitting upright, clinging to the phone with one hand, the dashboard with the other. "My partner and I were shot ... by a redhead ... in sunglasses ... and a track suit. He popped out of the trunk ... literally ... with a briefcase and a revolver ... and escaped in our vehicle."

Typing in the background.

"According to my records, you and your partner were assigned a Ford Chase electric four-door with license plate J411694."

"Correct."

More typing.

"Hang in there, Ms. Evans. The cavalry will arrive shortly."

Commander Ray Salvatore disconnects. Rudy becomes unbearably dizzy, opens the passenger door, and collapses into a ball on the ground. She lifts her head and gazes toward the raging fire along the Coastal Ranges. There, she notices a Liberator. From her distance, it appears to be a child's toy that has been tossed on a hill. While digging a trench, the robot suddenly retracts its shovel and slides it into a holster on its back. The majestic mech—with its red, white, and monochrome firefighting colors— turns in Rudy's direction. It runs, leaps into the air, and soars into the sky. Looming larger and larger as it approaches, the massive machine slows its descent with silent, rocket-like thrusters blasting from the soles of its feet. The giant robot touches down gently before Rudy, a towering silhouette etched in the radiant glow of the extraterrestrial veil.

Gazing up at the three-hundred-foot colossus, Rudy can hardly believe what she is seeing. The grisly, metallic face, with antennae protruding from its crown, peers down at her with its tenacious mandibles, smiling at the non-deceased F.B.I. agent.

"I AM LIBERATOR 6-2-A-3 WITH THE NORTH AMERICAN INTERGOVERNMENTAL TASK FORCE CLIMATE DIVISION," bellows the mech. The right arm of the bot rises slightly, aimed at the woman. "FIELD AGENT RUDY EVANS, I AM AUTHORIZED TO INFORM YOU THAT YOU ARE HEREBY RELIEVED FROM ACTIVE DUTY WITH THE FEDERAL BUREAU OF INVESTIGATION AND PLACED ON MEDICAL LEAVE."

There's a shot from the mech's arm, and a white parachute extends over a gurney that floats down to Rudy. Upon landing, the parachute deflates, and a dozen mechanical legs unfold from the medical bed, positioning it next to the shooting victim. The spidery limbs hoist the F.B.I. agent up from the ground, lay her onto the gurney, and wrap her in a protective blanket. After a preliminary bio scan and round of medical injections, she is cleared for takeoff. The limbs of the medical bed transform into propellers, and the injured detective is whisked away by the emergency drone. Rudy's last recollection of her rescue is the Liberator saying farewell as she is airlifted to a hospital.

"GOODBYE, MISS EVANS!" the enormous mech bellows with a friendly wave. "THE UNITED STATES OF AMERICA AND REPUBLIC OF CALIFORNIA ARE GRATEFUL FOR YOUR SERVICE!"

Part 2
They Feed on Your Fear

Chapter 11

Pizza. Although the comfort food is intended to ease the anxiety, fear, and depression of campers and counselors, it does little to improve morale. The first supper at Friendly Forest after the *Kiaski* invasion, held in a chow hall filled with two-hundred children and adults, unfolds in an atmosphere of dread.

"Try the seasoning," whispers the cook, a gangly figure covered by an apron and tattoos. He tips the shaker towards Myles's plate. "Garlic, oregano, and a few secret ingredients for extra kick." He winks. "You look like you could use some spice in your life, my friend."

"Right now, I'm just grateful to *have* a life," Myles says, surrendering his plate. The cook dowses his slice of cheese pizza with the fiery flakes and sends him off with a meal and drink.

It's difficult to appreciate the man's positivity, Myles thinks as he finds a seat. *Is the cook a local, unaffected by the assault upon the largest city along the West Coast? The expats also seem immune to the crisis.*

"My parents died years ago," says Richard, munching on a slice of pepperoni pizza. "There's just my aunt and uncle for me to look after. So far, they say, there have been no *Kiaski* sightings off the coast of Sydney."

"Let's hope it stays that way," says Matt, biting a slice of olive pizza. "My brother says no space dogs have been reported yet paddling to Liverpool. I'm wondering if this alien assault is an isolated incident."

"That's just because extraterrestrials aren't interested in your boring destinations," Scott says. "New Zealand, on the other hand, now *there* is beautiful terrain any species in the universe would love to ravage."

An exchange of glances and half-hearted chuckles.

"All of you making international calls," Myles wonders out loud, "and none of you had trouble with reception?"

"Huh," Scott says. "I'm not following you."

"You would think with an alien attack underway," Myles explains, "satellite signals would be disrupted ... lines busy ... devices not connecting."

Members of the hivemind collectively shrug.

"There were no communication issues for me," Matt says. "Although now that you mention it, when I logged onto the net, the screen did have a strange glow."

"Glow?"

"That's right, a fuzz around the monitor, like that light when we were standing in the forest," Richard says, glancing at Geo and José. "You know, after the fight."

Stange, Myles thinks. *They are seeing it, too, when they first focus on a screen. Has the camp been fed magic mushrooms? Is that the 'kick' that the chef has been adding to our food? The kind that tunes us into the Space Invaders Broadcasting Channel?*

No time to discuss. Overhearing mention of the fight, José lowers his head, withdrawing deeper into himself as he chomps on a slice of pineapple pizza. Geo, standing in earshot of the expats, assumes damage control and mutes the conversation.

"Excuse me, ladies and gentlemen!" he hollers at the traumatized crowd. "Are you enjoying your dinner?"

Lackluster nods.

"Glad to hear it," he says, projecting unwarranted optimism. "Jeanie would like to share a few words."

Instead of the usual applause, silence follows Jeanie's introduction. The camp leader dabbles her mouth with a napkin and rises from her seat. If anyone wonders about the toll that the *Kiaski* invasion has had on civilization, poor Jeanie is all the proof that is necessary. She looks like she's aged a decade in an afternoon. Swaths of her golden hair seem to have transformed to silvery gray. The few wrinkles that once graced her face have exploded into a patchwork of fault lines. Even her pupils, from the fatigue of crisis management, have expanded to resemble captive black holes. In essence, Jeanie shows on the surface what Myles—and many of his peers, he suspects—feel inside: helplessness.

"For those of you who have loved ones that are alive … you will be released as soon as they arrive to get you," she says. Judging by the silence, the number of campers who have parents coming to retrieve them are few. "For those of you whose loved ones are … no longer among the living … you can consider us your family now. I know none of the counselors, nor I, could ever make up for the loss you *feel*—"

Mention of the word 'feel' prompts an explosive wave of emotion. Around the cafeteria, children burst into tears. Their sadness swells like a rising tide, drowning out Jeanie's voice and the fragile order of the camp. Her final remarks are strained and barely distinguishable among the wailing. "Let's just sit and cry together, and for those who don't want to cry, we can sing. Geo, please—"

Geo scrambles to the utility closet. He withdraws his guitar, takes position in front of Jeanie and the rest of the crowd, and strums the instrument. In the warm glow of incandescent light in the dining hall, the cuts and bruises he endured from the fistfight with José appear to be almost gone. It's as if the scrap never happened, and the incident, along with their whole lives before the alien spaceship crash landed, had been imagined.

This subtle observation—this shift in reality—sends a shiver up Myles's spine.

"Hopefully many of you know this tune by now," Geo says, his award-winning grin returned to his face.

He proceeds. "There was a tree."

A few dreadful responses. "There was a tree."

"That loved to sing."

A few lackluster responses. "That loved to sing."

As Geo sings, the children's cries slowly transform to song—sad, clear, and exalting to the ear—a cleansing deluge for the troubled mind.

"The prettiest hole!"

"The prettiest hole!"

"That you ever did see!"

"That you ever did see!"

Myles is swept away by a torrent of youthful spirit. Suddenly, no challenge seems so great, no obstacle so overwhelming, that together those gathered around him cannot overcome. While this sentiment is important, he realizes faith in each other may not be enough. As the campers and counselors finish singing and part ways for the night, Myles realizes that to survive any trials and tribulations ahead, it would require a whole new level of teamwork—and far fewer fist fights.

An exhaustion so deep, it's like dragging himself out of a sinkhole.

"Pst!" José whispers, shaking Myles's shoulder. "Get up, homie."

Myles rolls in bed toward a moonbeam shining through a crack in the cabin door. "I had a nightmare that aliens devoured my ..."

He doesn't finish his sentence, seized by the anguish of his torn heart.

"Let's go," whispers Myles's shadowy friend, squatting next to him. "You need to see this."

Groggily, Myles assesses the other campers. White sheets rise and fall from the cots like breathing ghosts. Judging by the snores, the children of *Whispering Dreams* are sound asleep, leaving Myles jealous, but free, to step away from them. He fumbles for his sneakers and stumbles toward José. Outside is not as peaceful as his previous nocturnal adventure. In the distance, the *Chill Room*'s lights draw eyes and flies. A steady stream of staff trickles from all parts of camp toward the building.

"What now?" Myles asks.

José's eyes, hidden beneath the glow of the moonlight, reveal more darkness than clarity.

"The President's about to speak."

"I thought we were done watching the news."

"Jeanie hasn't left the *Chill Room* since we ate dinner," he says, leading the way. "Apparently, the war with the aliens isn't going well. I spent the last fifteen minutes rounding up the entire staff. I let you sleep the longest."

"Thanks."

Again, it's standing room only at the only place in camp that offers access to the outside world. Jeanie is fixed on a stool, remote in hand, as a grumbling crowd elbows for the best view. José and Myles cram into a corner next to Tiffany.

"Good morning," Myles says.

"Not really," Tiffany says, yawning as she sips a cup of coffee.

Projecting onto the monitors is the Great Seal of the United States. The seal contains a bald eagle with a shield that closely resembles the American flag covering the bird's abdomen. The bird's white-feathered head is turned away from the arrows it clenches with its left talons, instead turned toward an olive branch it clenches with its right talons. As Myles recalls from school, the bald eagle's orientation toward the olive branch symbolizes the nation's preference for peace.

Not today. The monitors that display the Great Seal cut to a live video of President Leandro Benítez, seated at his desk in the Oval Office. The leathery-skinned octogenarian, with beady eyes and a charcoal toupee, struggles to mask his senility and disdain for a rotting country.

"This great nation has endured many challenges since it was forged together, two-hundred-and-sixty years ago, to resist tyranny," says the Commander-in-Chief, wads of spittle spraying from his mouth. "The American Revolution, which started as a tax revolt in 1776, led to uprisings around the world against the British Empire and its overreaching government. In the United States, we managed to set a new standard for a liberated society, but unfortunately, freedom was not a right granted to all people. The Civil War that erupted in 1861 prompted our nation to focus inward, and reflect on our ideals, as the blood of our brothers and sisters spilled. Slavery was ultimately abolished, and however resistant, the South was forced to remain part of the Union—kicking and crying foul through the twenty-first century. Two World Wars and a much longer Cold War ended the spread of fascism and communism worldwide, paving the way for democratic capitalism to prevail as the dominant global political and economic system of our time. However, these developments did not mean peace was secure in our own continent ..."

President Benítez pauses to sip a glass of water. For a moment, there is a surreal twinkle in his eyes, a pixelated glitch spiraling out from the monitors, almost tickling the brains of the Friendly Forest staff, who appear spellbound, Myles notices. The Commander-In-Chief wipes his mouth with the sleeve of his suit and sighs, refreshed and revitalized, as if the old fart just took a sip from the fountain of youth.

"With our nation's successes, we also acknowledge its failures," says the President, gazing at the teleprompter. "The thirst for freedom, it turns out, is endless, and difficult to quench in a society as vast and diverse as our own. Regional divisions in perspectives and values have led to irreconcilable differences among our people. Instead of plundering this nation into another Civil War, however, our federal leadership has had the wisdom to create new opportunities for greater, and more customized, regional self-governance."

President Benítez rubs his eyes, yawns. So much for the fountain of youth. His sleepy gaze, and hypnotic speech, resumes.

"Today, the United States consists of a paternalistic federal system and semi-autonomous regions—its children, so to speak—with varying abilities and needs," he says. "We have, for example, allowed the establishment of the Independent Stronghold of Texas, where in exchange for paying a higher federal tax rate, the oil industry has been permitted to run its course until the wells run dry, a haven of rugged individualism where boys can be boys, men can be men, and an abortion must be approved by the father of a fetus for it to be legal."

President Benítez grins, revealing a set of bright, beautiful dentures. His tongue playfully rolls along the ridge of his mouth.

"We also have New New York," he says, "a conglomeration of eastern states and their population of well-heeled elites economically tied to the boom-and-bust cycles of the finance industry. This concentration of over-educated and under-armed citizens treat men, women, and gender non-specific individuals equally under the laws and traditions of their land. Although they are extensive contributors to climate change, they are also committed to saving the Earth from further destruction. Like the Independent Stronghold of Texas, the people of New New York provide the federal government with substantial tax support in exchange for the privilege of being able to manage their own affairs and enjoy their unique culture, freedom, and heritage."

President Benítez takes a deep breath and persists. "Of course, there is also The Heartland, often referred to as Farm Country, where the worst problems involve volatile weather, flooded fields, tornadoes, and ultra-hot summers that often lead to contaminated, diseased, and decreased food supplies. Otherwise, the fine folks of this region are known to enjoy a centered and stable—if not somewhat sheltered and isolated—way of life."

President Benitez shifts in his seat until he is comfortable. "Of course, I dare not forget to recognize the former states known as the Southern Confederation, where Dixie music plays loudly and proudly in the streets, fried food remains the penultimate cuisine, and many political leaders long to rewind the clock, eliminate equality, and return the region to its pre-Civil War 'glory.' Perhaps the Southern Confederation's greatest threat to democracy, besides themselves, are the horrendous hurricanes and dangerous weather patterns exacerbated by climate change with which they must contend. Compromise is sometimes necessary to prevent strife, and so the Southern Confederation's body of elected ministers and armed laymen have promised not to force their values and way of life on their affluent New New York neighbors to the north so long as the region's stifling economy continues to be subsidized by the federal government and support its large population of rural, poor, and poorly educated households."

President Benítez takes another sip of water. He sits upright with a jolt of enthusiasm. His pupils dilate, shiny and lustrous, as the pace of his speech increases with a renewed focus.

"Finally, there is the Alliance of Western States," he says, "a mixture of conservative and liberal bastions, such as Arizona and Oregon, that cooperate out of mutual self-interest to combat the unique challenges foisted on them from a rapidly deteriorating environment—chronic droughts, wildfires, and expanding deserts that have prompted them to launch a war against the land, instead of a war against each other, to maximize the resources they need for their survival. Breakthroughs in solar and nuclear energy, increased water-retainment and fire-suppression techniques, and a new era of public-private partnerships are underway in the Alliance of Western States to maintain a high quality of life for the citizens who reside there."

President Benítez's eyes roll and return to the teleprompter. He settles on the camera and waits for a moment, as if making sure he still has the world's attention.

"That is how this great nation has adapted to change during this century—by recognizing our differences and decentralizing federal power to preserve the peace, dignity, and stability of North America as a whole," he says. He coughs, withdraws a handkerchief from his suit pocket, and hacks into it violently. After clearing his throat, he resumes. "The federal government leverages its national influence through tax collection and subsidies, and in exchange for loyalty to this Union, regions are permitted to manage themselves and their climate-related problems the way they see best. Is it a perfect system? No. But it works, and it provides context for what I am about to say next."

The sparkling optimism in President Benítez's eyes as he spoke about the Western Alliance of States—and the possibility of peace, cooperation, and progress— fades as his pupils transform into portals of despair.

"No region, perhaps, offers a more unique contribution to this great nation than the Republic of California," he says, suppressing fear in his eyes with a smile. "Their Eco-Socialist leadership has ambitious plans to improve a depleting landscape, declining property values, and draining tax coffers through a series of bold initiatives. For example, California's very own space program—The Heaven Project—is determined to apply advances in technology that scientists expect to gain from the colonization of outer space toward Earth's development. California's goal to overcome climate change and income inequality by instituting sustainable environmental and economic practices, is admirable and endearing, even if, at this moment, such promises mostly remain a dream ..."

President Benítez's smile disappears as he proceeds to cough horrifically. Finally, he regains self-control. "Unfortunately, there is a new threat to Southern California, poised to not only topple their fledgling Republic, but destroy the entirety of North America."

The image on the monitors cut to drone footage over the financial district of downtown Los Angeles. The bird's eye view, several hundred feet above a street, shows structure fires billowing from sleek, mirrored banks, bumper-to-bumper car wrecks, and half-eaten people strewn on sidewalks. A convoy of soldiers in a personnel truck unload behind an upturned tree and set up a gatling gun. As they do, *Kiaskis* emerge from shattered storefront windows, stairways, and dark spaces as if smelling the vulnerable defenders. Before the large gun fires, the insatiable dogs from outer space pounce on the soldiers. Growls, screams, and shots ring out as the platoon is devoured.

The drone heads upward, panning away from the scene as President Benítez continues his address. "The *Kiaskis* arrived on a ship that crash landed off the coast of California, near San Diego, at 2:35 Pacific Daylight Time yesterday afternoon. As you can see from footage, within hours of their arrival, the results have been devastating."

The bird's eye view expands to include several more streets. Among the city's towering edifices, a military-grade Liberator touches down in Pershing Square. The heavily armored, A.I.-piloted machine has a shielded head crowned with antennae and horns. Myles once read it is made with saginium sheets, with a wire-mesh jessinium overlay, that protects a condensed nuclear fuel cell at the heart of the beast. The Liberator's bulging shoulders and arms bristle with sensors and weapons, missile launchers and heavy-caliber machine guns, leading to hands with long, precise robotic fingers said to be able to lift, crush, and cut through a bus. An advanced hydraulic system supports the mech's legs, wrapped in a polymer-coated tank tread and huge, talon-like feet.

"Look at that monster," José says. "We'll see who has the upper hand now."

Waves of *Kiaskis* converge from surrounding streets. The silvery mech, glistening in the L.A. sunlight like a giant knight in shining armor, unleashes a barrage of Hellfire missiles, tracers, and high-caliber gun fire that explode with a firework-like brilliance and splatter neon-red alien blood everywhere. There is a collective sigh in the *Chill Room* as Friendly Forest staff watch the gigantic machine push back the tide of cosmic canines with stunning success.

"Hell, yeah!" shouts José, giving Myles a slap on the shoulder. "America is pulling through."

The victory, however, is short-lived. *Kiaskis* burst from sidewalk drains and street sewers near the base of the bot, leaping off the ground and scrambling onto the mech with their claws. Scaling the mech's legs, torso, and arms, they tear through the protective layers of metal with their razor-sharp teeth, ripping out wires, confusing and disorienting the giant death dealer long enough for it to relent its attack and provide an opportunity for more *Kiaskis* to break through the wall of murderous bullets and explosions. The Liberator flails its arms and legs, desperately trying to shake off the space invaders. *Kiaskis* wriggle their way into the sentinel's joints, penetrating its mainframe and internal systems like an army of ants overwhelming a morsel of chocolate. External displays blink faulty as guns and missiles misfire, and the mech seizes mid-stride, crashing through a high-rise, sending dust and debris into the air.

When the grimy cloud clears, the Liberator is seen in a crouched position. Its rear engines ignite, legs extend, and it propels off the ground, hovering briefly, uncertainly, as its corrupted internal systems struggle.

"The *Kiaskis* prefer flesh, but the fact is, they'll attack anything they deem sentient," says the President, whose eyes appear heavy, gaze sullen with defeat. "They can swim, dash, jump. The only thing they cannot do is fly, so the only place that is safe to be in Southern California right now, is far above it."

The drone footage shows *Kiaskis* bursting through the eyes and mouth of the Liberator. The mech, no longer operational, falls to the ground with a thundering crash, sending more dirt and dust into the air, a final busted and rusted signal of surrender.

"We have no idea how many arrived on their ship," says the Commander-In-Chief, and the view on the net returns to him seated at his desk in the Oval Office. "Since the first swarm landed on Southern California's beaches, however, they seem to have somehow multiplied their armies many times over. We estimate their numbers are now swelling in the tens of millions. Between our casualties and their inexplicable means of proliferation, we project that they are minutes away from overtaking the human population in Los Angeles, San Bernadino, Orange, and San Diego counties."

President Benítez's flopping toupee and ancient, sagging skin are no longer marks of an enduring leader but reflect the awful truth of a nation that is no longer equipped to save its own citizens from an alien invasion or the vagaries of their own government.

"It is due to these tragic circumstances and the overwhelming threat that the *Kiaskis* pose to the human race," he reads with quivering lips from the teleprompter, "that I have decided it is time to destroy this enemy once and for all. To save 300 million American lives, regretfully, I must sacrifice 30 million."

The monitors cut to the drone's view, now encompassing a vast swath over Los Angeles. The downed Liberator, along with several others that are positioned across the city, explode in succession, forming a line of fiery orange mushroom clouds. In addition, streaks of incoming missiles rain on America's largest sprawling metropolis, incinerating Southern California in a flash of light. The image on the monitors turns black as the electromagnetic pulse from multiple nuclear blasts reverberates from the City of Angels to the *Chill Room*, disrupting equipment.

Some counselors stare at blank screens. Some shake their heads in disgust and disbelief. Others burst into tears. Myles dashes outside, gasps, and takes several deep breaths of fresh mountain air. The sweet scent of pine, wildflower, and detritus lifts his spirits enough to lead his gaze upward.

A fiery glow, like a misplaced sunrise, simmers on the horizon where the scorched ruins of Southern California remain. The rest of the sky continues to twinkle, as dark and mysterious as always. The stars above, Myles's guide to reality, remain fixed and steady, shining down on him and the rest of humanity.

There must be more to life than the destruction and death caused by the *Kiaskis*. If only Myles could be up there, in space, exploring the heavens, and far from the nightmare-inducing hell these alien invaders have unleashed on Earth.

Chapter 12

"Easy on the clutch," Al says, lounging in his robe on a shiny recliner, watching a holographic baseball game projected on his lap. "There's a little drag when you switch from light speed back to neutral. If you're not careful, you'll grind the hyperdrive engine."

"Thanks," Myles says, kicking a controller with his left leg, pulling a lever with his right hand, part of the peculiar ballet of using a manual transmission to fly across the cosmos. "I'm just glad you and your unsolicited advice were able to join me on this trip."

As Myles downshifts, there is a loud thud that echoes through the hull of the spaceship. The streaks of neon flashing across the cockpit display dissipate, and their destination comes into view as they slow into neutral.

"Still a little rough, Myles," Mom says, lounging in floral pajamas in another recliner, glancing up from a crossword puzzle. "You need more practice with your interstellar flights, Boo. It's not like driving a car—"

"Can we just appreciate for a moment where we are, and how far we've come?" Myles says, pointing. "I mean … look!"

They gaze out from the cockpit display at a lime glow puncturing the black emptiness of space and smothered with blueberry and strawberry swirls.

"It looks like a sundae," Mom says, plugging a word into a line.

"That's Orion's Belt," Al says, pausing the baseball game with a clap of his hands, peering in awe at the spectacle through his spectacles. "One of the Seven Wonders of the Milky Way Galaxy. And lucky us, it is filled with habitable planets." He adds under his breath, "Are you kidding, Myles? I wouldn't miss this trip for the world."

"Good," Myles says, feeling nostalgic, "because right now our world is about the only thing I'm missing. I wish we could return to Earth."

Mom tosses the crossword toward her son. It floats to the front of his face.

"What's a seven-letter word for a race of carnivorous aliens?" she asks.

"Like, the reason we fled our planet?" Al asks. "That's not a nice question, is it, dear?"

There's a growl, and Myles glances back and finds a cluster of crimson eyes glaring at him from the dark corner of the cockpit. His stepfather and mother don't notice, or don't want to notice, the intruder.

Myles reads the line his mother plugged into the crossword: K-I-A-S-K-I-S, but he dares not say it out loud.

"I got this," he says, changing the word and sending the crossword back to his mom. "There is *no* race of carnivorous aliens. The correct answer is, N-O-T-H-I-N-G."

"Bingo!" Mom says, brimming with joy.

The crossword vanishes, and holographic confetti rains through the cockpit. "CONGRATULATIONS, HARPER FAMILY!" the ship's computer announces. "YOU BEAT 99% OF SUBSCRIBERS TO TODAY'S EDITION OF THE NEW NEW YORK TIMES CROSSWORD PUZZLE! ENJOY YOUR GALAXY GETAWAY!"

Myles shifts the engine into first gear, and he and his parents gaze in wonder as the ship slowly cruises toward a star-studded paradise.

Myles is startled awake, sweaty and disoriented from a dream which, with every conscious breath, slips further from his memory. *For a moment, my parents were alive, and we were free from this horrifying reality.* Lying in his bunk, he opens his eyes and stares up, not at the cosmos, but at the underside of the bunk above his, feeling a profound sense of grief and longing for his loved ones.

He turns and finds an empty plastic bottle lying on the floor. He reaches down and picks it up. *Decades of us standing by during an environmental catastrophe that we created hasn't improved our survival skills. Even if the nukes managed to wipe the Kiaskis off the map, who will really save us in the long run?*

He tosses the bottle into a recycling bin—score! Ali, Frank, and Sam are huddled in the corner playing cards.

"Why was the vampire so nervous about his poker game?" Ali asks.

"I don't know, why?" Frank says.

"His opponent was *raising the stakes.*"

"Ha, ha," Sam says.

They glance sideways at their counselor.

"Hey, Myles."

"Hey, guys."

Trying to resume normal life after a nuclear strike against an extraterrestrial horde was not on anyone's bingo card when they arrived at Camp Friendly Forest. Today, no electronic rooster rallies staff and children to their feet. There is no morning meeting in the amphitheater. No structure. No routine. Hell, no civilization.

Light from the sun peeks through the cabin door. Myles's feet slide into his sneakers and lead him to the great outdoors. While the sun remains anonymous, hidden behind the towering redwoods, its rays illuminate the branches a golden greenish hue, leaving the counselor to guess the time must be around noon. The only indication of a massive blast to the south is a smokey haze visible in that direction, easily confused with the usual pollution caused by smog and wildfires. At least catching up on sleep has allowed Myles's an opportunity to refresh his mind and compartmentalize his dread, and the scene at Friendly Forest appears similarly upbeat, as if staff and children collectively decided to languish in the eye of the storm and enjoy a reprieve from their shared nightmare.

Jays and nutcrackers dart from branch to branch, competing for love and attention. Their song and dance are a pleasant reminder that not all dramas are dark and perilous. In fact, many lead to new life. Children run wild, unorganized and unsupervised, full of laughter and mirth, as teenagers gathered in the amphitheater pair off and kiss. They wave at Myles in an over-friendly manner as he passes, as if to assure him nothing is odd about the erotically charged game of truth-or-dare they play amid the crumbling façade of their world. Myles waves back at them, polite, not questioning otherwise.

The cafeteria staff, on indefinite hiatus, have abandoned their posts, leaving hungry and thirsty campers to forge for grub on their own. Instead of long lines, trays, and food handlers, the new policy seems to be, fend for yourself. At least power has been restored to the dining hall, perhaps from back-up generators.

Myles fills a cup of coffee from the self-serve station and nods at a group of counselors seated at a table. They strike him as chatty rats, whispering to each other conspiratorially as they sip their dark brew. The rats don't acknowledge him, and since he is the youngest and least experienced of the counselor-rodents, this second-class treatment is something he has come to accept, even in a post-*Kiaski* universe. The urge to fight back is becoming stronger, however, because he's starting to realize that fighting back is all he can do.

"Choose your battles," Al reminds him.

"I should have listened to you more when you were alive."

"Better late than never," his stepfather says with a grin, sipping coffee at the table, wedged between the over-sized vermin.

"Let's enjoy moments together like these more often."

"That's the spirit, son."

Myles exits the dining hall with a brimming cup. A barefoot girl wearing a bikini top, shorts, and a pirate patch draped over her left eye sprints past him waving a tomahawk.

"What are you *doing* with *that*?" he yells.

"Nothing!" she shouts. She pulls her tiny arm back and flings the handle. The blade whirls through the air, over a thicket of bushes, and shatters a soda bottle propped on top of a tree stump.

"Nice throw," Myles admits. "What's your name, miss?"

"Kylie."

"Where'd you get that tomahawk?"

Last time Myles checked, they were locked in a shed. Kylie giggles and scampers toward a group of boys and girls, each armed with BB-guns. When they see Myles, they dart through the bushes and disappear like mischievous fairies into the woods. Apparently, the inmates have taken over the asylum. No sign of Jeanie, Geo, nor senior staff redirecting these liberated juveniles into safe, structured activities. The horses, usually stabled, roam the soccer field. Someone needs to get this place in check.

Myles embarks on a quest to find grown-ups in charge, whistling "Green Grass Grows All Around" on his way to the *Chill Room*. Only, it's not called that anymore. The big bold letters engraved in a wood slab are listed as *Command Center*. Myles blinks to make sure what he is seeing is correct. His eyes do not appear to be lying. Who made the change, and why? Another mysterious distortion of reality since the *Kiaskis* arrived.

Stepping inside, the monitors remain blank, but Myles hears the harsh staccato of a news broadcaster rattling off updates about the alien invasion.

For a moment, he surveys the room, seeking the source of the information. That's when he realizes he's not alone. Sitting in front of him, like a chameleon blending in with her surroundings, is Jeanie. She's in the same position he and the other counselors left her in the night before. He leans to his side and notices a transistor radio situated upright on a table in front of her. He remains standing behind her, not wanting to disturb her, as he listens to the news.

"By destroying Los Angeles, Orange, San Bernardino, and San Diego counties with a pre-emptive nuclear strike, federal officials said that they hope they have eliminated the *Kiaski* threat to North America. In case the threat persists, however, military forces are mobilizing in the Mojave Desert outside the irradiated zones. This strategic deployment of ground and air forces is intended to prevent any remnants of the extraterrestrial menace from spreading to Arizona, Nevada, Northern California, and the rest of the United States ..."

As the news broadcast continues, Myles feels the sadness he's struggled to suppress transforming into something else ... a kind of hate.

"When federal officials were asked if they would resort to using more nuclear weapons if the *Kiaski* threat persists, they declined to comment."

"Brilliant!" Myles bursts, slamming hand on table. "If the first round of nukes doesn't force the *Kiaskis* into oblivion, maybe more nukes will!" He steps next to Jeanie, directing his verbal onslaught at the radio. "We'll just keep on blowing off chunks of North America until there's nothing left to destroy!"

Jeanie, however, seems unimpressed with Myles's diatribe. She doesn't even acknowledge him.

"I'm sorry, I can be a little insensitive at times," the counselor says, too embarrassed to face her. "This alien takeover is crazy, and I apologize if my comments have offended you, ma'am. Sarcasm helps me cope with depressing news, I guess."

Jeanie continues to ignore him. Finally, he turns toward her. "Look, if this is about the fight yesterday with Geo and José, I promise, I was only trying—"

Her eyes are half open. The way she sits upright, with such impeccable posture, reminds him of someone meditating. "Miss Scruggs, am I *disturbing* you?"

Still, she doesn't respond. Annoyed with the broadcaster's white noise, he turns off the radio and focuses on the owner of Camp Friendly Forest. Breathing. But this isn't meditation. Country women don't dabble in the Eastern arts, do they? Myles snaps his fingers in front of her face. Nothing. Her pupils, however, oscillate beneath her eyelids.

Are you sleeping?

Where is your mind?

What took you away from us?

Jeanie doesn't reply, verbally or otherwise. Questions about her state of being, however, make Myles's head spin. He glances down and sees that she is sitting in a crusty pool of vomit. He looks up and notices a trickle of bile dribbling from her lips. He clasps his hands on a table and holds himself upright, breathing slowly, deliberately, trying to prevent himself from succumbing to nausea.

She'll be fine.

We'll be fine.

I just need to keep my head together, for the kids.

Myles stumbles from the *Command Center*. The farther removed he is from unconscious Jeanie, the better he feels.

Chapter 13

While most civilians think of mechs as strictly A.I. bots, all mechs ae designed to accommodate a pilot should one be necessary. Military regulations prevent Commander Ray Salvatore from carrying non-combat related items into the cockpit of his Liberator. Included are personal property as seemingly benign as chewing gum to more coveted belongings, such as wedding rings.

Although Ray's only child, Sara, is now an adult, their relationship as she grew up came with an accumulation of effects the distinguished officer still holds dear. Some of these items, in an ideal world, Ray would bring with him aboard his mech into battle, reminders of that which he values most in this world: her. Among the objects, clay figures Sara made of her father, mother, and herself when she was four. She gave them to Ray following his return from a tour in the Middle East, to celebrate his homecoming, and her remarkable eye surgery that cured her color blindness.

In addition, there are bracelets, cards and drawings Sara made for her father over the course of his military service which the commander, known among his peers as a divorced but devout family man, keeps on display in his Phoenix home. The figurines, jewelry, notes, and other memorabilia that he saves celebrates Sara's life, chronicle milestones of her development, and reflect the timeless adoration he will always have for his daughter. This remains the case, despite the fact Sara's mother left Ray more than a decade ago—and Sara herself, a college art student—is fully grown and appears quite different from his 'baby girl' of yesteryear.

Thus, for a dad and daughter who have always been close emotionally, but not always close to each other in proximity, Ray's regard for Sara provides meaning to his life in ways that busting America's bad guys does not. Being in touch with that meaning is important because the commander, regarded by many as an 'army of one,' often works alone and must rely on his wits to maintain motivation, and sanity, in securing successful outcomes for the North American Intergovernmental Task Force Security Division.

Approaching fifty and responsible for organizing NAITFSD's special operations, Ray also serves as the agency's primary operative, leading the missions he determines necessary for the safety and security of the continent. The extreme leadership demands placed on him are due, in part, to his exceptional experience in the field as well as his skill piloting the Liberator. It's as if man and machine were built for one another. In fact, some familiar with the origins of the mech might argue that is the case. They say the commander is the beneficiary of a technology that is, ultimately, otherworldly in its nature.

Ray never indulges such rumors. Whenever he leaves home on a mission, the item he brings with him that reminds him *why* he continues to serve his country after waging so many perilous wars on its behalf, boils down to one single digital photo that is permitted aboard his mech.

"ACE, show me my favorite picture."

"Yes, boss," says the Lib's Artificial Co-Pilot Enhancement. The visual display before Ray switches from a real-time overlay of a rural California town, wherein lies his target, to a digital photo of Sara Salvatore. The picture depicts a small child with the same striking grayish eyes as her father, taken after he completed his tour in Iran as captain of an elite squad of Liberators during the Oil Wars.

This photo of Sara, shot by a military communications officer as Ray spoke to the press about the Middle East operation's 'limited success,' became ingrained in his consciousness because of the unbridled joy it reveals—specifically, his daughter's beaming smile as she gazes up at him, seeing him for the first time in crisp, full color. The grin on Sara's face, standing among a throng of reporters, is unlike anything Ray has ever seen, before or since, a reflection of youthful optimism and a blind happiness for life's possibilities. How glad Sara was to see him then, and how fortunate Ray remains, now to have her in his life.

Even from afar. Because for Ray, such a photo makes his purpose clear. The madness of this existence not only brings destruction and death, but it also delivers beauty and creativity through which even the worst shades of reality sometimes prove wonderful. Before he begins any military operation, admiring the photo of Sara taken during one of the darkest days in his career, tends to make Ray weepy and help him to reaffirm his single greatest conviction: *There is always a reason to safeguard a world based in hope.*

"Would you like a box of tissue?" ACE asks playfully.

"Very funny," Ray says. He instinctively reaches up to wipe the tears from his eyes, but his sensor-filled helmet beats him to it, sucking the salty moisture from his face to ensure he maintains maximum visual clarity and hand-eye coordination. "I think all I need is little less lip from my computer."

"Ha, ha," says ACE with the usual glib. "Now, *that* is funny. You are becoming more amusing in your old age, commander." The light tone of their conversation pivots: "Movement detected at the target's location. Would you like to take a closer look?"

"Yes, please."

The image of Sara's beaming smile dissolves into a pixelated puff, replaced by the real-time overlay of Oro Loma, an unincorporated area off the Interstate 5 Freeway, forty-five miles north of the extraterrestrial anomaly that manifested itself at 2:35 p.m. yesterday along with the last known whereabouts of Alice Walker. A night's worth of drone and satellite reconnaissance activity, led by the artificially intelligent computers at Ray's disposal, traced the stolen sedan with Department of Justice plates to a lone inn located in the small farming community. A series of hacks into the messages of a tracked laptop confirm that the individual responsible for abducting the psychic and her accomplices, as well as murdering one F.B.I. field officer and critically wounding another, occupies Room 5 of the Sierra View Motel.

"Daddy's Girl, take me home," Ray says, and the software system that runs ACE zooms past the stolen sedan parked in the inn's lot and provides a closer view of the occupied motel room. "Nice, but I ain't home yet."

Ray struggles to see through a window frame partially blocked by a dangling curtain. His attention is registered by his helmet, which causes the view in the cockpit to amplify, zooming in much closer.

"Better."

From two miles away, the commander identifies Alice Walker lying in a bed, supine and unconscious. Next to her is Henrik Gustavo, waking from sleep. Propped above him is a bot, and based on the reports Ray read, presumably this is the antagonistic sidekick Mr. Pootin. Out of view but detected by bio-scan is Ray's target. He is sitting at a table, typing on a laptop. His messages are being decoded by Daddy's Girl in real time as they are transmitted to the Kremlin.

"The target is preparing to relocate, but it is not clear how or where," ACE relays to the commander. "Judging by the minimal information that is being communicated to his superiors, he is also probably aware that he is being monitored."

"He'll move soon," the commander agrees, squeezing his hands. His haptic gloves crackle as his palms flex, knuckles protrude, and his black body suit cools his skin in response to his slightly elevated heart rate. The electro-statically charged gelatinous insulation that secures the commander inside the cockpit oxidizes, freeing his limbs for maximum mobility as smart threads—a neural relay that crisscrosses the pilot's arms, legs, and head—helps Daddy's Girl anticipate the commander's motives and moves. As Ray focuses on the scene, the crack between the window frame and curtain expands further across the capsule shield, revealing the assassin's face as he peeks outside from the motel room window. Ray watches him assess the position of his Liberator along with circling helicopter and drones.

"Shit," Ray says, the inflection of his voice vacillating just enough for Daddy's Girl to register fear.

"What's the problem, commander?" ACE asks.

At any time, under any circumstances, no matter what the guise, Ray Salvatore would be able to recognize the dark eyes of death, the bloody-colored hair, and the murderous jawline of his greatest foe.

"Our target is Herio Atta," he says. "Dressed like a clown in that track suit, but definitely him."

"The same assassin who abducted your ex-wife and daughter and attempted to murder them?"

"Yep," Ray says. "Thankfully, that courageous citizen, Chuck Shaw, successfully intervened …"

Ray still vividly recalls the incident as reported on the terrorist's stark resume. Although the two hostages were rescued, Atta's rampage in 2023 at a Flagstaff police station left a dozen officers dead. The incident is considered one of dozens of assassination plots connected to Atta, yet he has never been brought to justice.

"The guy's a ghost," Ray concedes. "His career, if you can call it that, started in his teens, and although he now couldn't be much older than thirty, I'm pretty sure he has single-handedly created more chaos around the globe than the Devil himself."

"Sounds like a worthy opponent," ACE says. "Perhaps it was fate that brought you together again?"

"Come on, ACE. You know I don't believe in miracles. More like a mathematical anomaly." For a moment, Ray feels his age in the form of a dull, inflexible ache in his lower back. "I just hope I still have what it takes to take him down."

"Of course, you do," ACE says. "You have *me*."

Ray takes a deep breath, clears his head, and the throbbing in his lower back subsides. *Mind over matter.*

"We need to be ready for anything and think outside our usual strategic parameters, ACE. Imagine a man as smart and resourceful as us, with youth on his side. A Liberator might not be enough to stop him."

"There you go with more jokes," ACE says. "You know, commander, we have enough firepower in our hull to obliterate a city."

"Our mission is to extract, not demolish," Ray says, careful not to budge and give Atta indication of the Liberator's heightened status. "However, *he* could easily turn this mission into mass destruction. We must tread carefully."

"Aye, sir."

Chapter 14

With Jeanie indisposed, the next in Camp Friendly Forest's chain of command is Geo, and Myles finds him bare-chested and in cutoff jean shorts, face shielded by a sombrero as he sips a bottle of tequila in the back of the company van.

"Nice hat," Myles says.

"Thanks," Geo says, ignoring the sarcasm. "You can find anything in that costume shed behind the amphitheater." He foists the bottle of urine-colored liquid onto the young counselor's hands. "Take a swig."

Myles cautiously accepts the invitation. He is unsure how to proceed with the difficult conversation he intends to have with Geo regarding *what the hell are we doing?* without further damaging the director's frail ego.

"Don't drink too much, or it'll make you sick," Geo warns with a grin as the acidic liquor splashes Myles's tongue. Instead of spitting it up, Myles swallows a mouthful, sending a high-octane jolt of fermented agave down his throat.

Might as well dive into the discomfort.

"Is that what made Jeanie catatonic?" the younger counselor asks, handing back the bottle. "She drank too much tequila?"

The grin on Geo's face drops.

"She let 'em get to her," he says with a sudden and unexpected sobriety contrary to his condition. He takes another swig and places the bottle on the floor of the van, stands, falters, and grips the top of the back doors with both hands, propping himself upright. He gazes at the trees and, finally, at the high school graduate he hired a month ago. "After the news about the nukes ... something changed in the old lady. It's like, she couldn't deal with the truth of what we've become."

"Yeah, and what's that?"

"Cowards," Geo says with a sigh. "While you and the rest of staff returned to bed sulking about the end of the world, Jeanie insisted on staying awake and keeping up with the news. Even though we had no power, and the monitors didn't work, she found that old transistor radio, some batteries, and a station that provided her with updates. I stopped pretending to care about keeping my job, and eventually followed the rest of you to bed. When I woke this morning, I found her there in that trance, and that's when I realized ..."

Geo's eyes waver, as if he's fighting off an urge to take a nap.

"Realized *what*?" Myles asks, demanding that he stay awake.

"It's a *mind job*," Geo mumbles, grabbing the bottle of tequila. "They're playing with our heads, dude. Jeanie is the toughest person I know, and if she has succumbed to the fear, it's only a matter of time before the rest of us do."

"Fear," Myles says, struggling to say the word out loud. "You make it sound ... contagious."

Geo stumbles with the bottle of tequila through the dusty camp parking lot toward the forest, spinning in circles. When he stops spinning, his direction is reoriented toward the camp. "I'm not wasting any more time ... if we're going to die ... I'm going to make out with a broad on the way to hell ..."

He wanders off toward the cabins.

"Man, what is that *pendejo's* problem?" José asks.

Myles turns and finds his friend next to him. "What everyone's problem is. Unresolved family trauma?"

They laugh, clasp each other's shoulders, and head in the direction opposite Geo, toward the dining hall.

"You've seen Jeanie?"

"Uh-huh."

"What are we going to do?"

"Call a town meeting," José says. "Figure out a plan. And we need to do it in a Camp Friendly Forest way."

"Yeah," Myles agrees. "Show them a future that isn't *all* doom and gloom."

"A future worth fighting for," José agrees, finishing his friend's thought.

Myles is seized with an idea.

"An ice cream social!"

"A .... what?"

"If you wanted me to join Russia's cyberwarfare department, you could have just asked," Gus says, shifting in bed to avoid the stabbing pain in his shoulder and leg. "Loading my body with bullets is not as motivating to me as putting dollars into my bank account."

"The Russians don't pay in dollars," says the assassin, peeking through the curtain, gazing outside the window. "In Russia, they pay in *id*."

"Of course, an authoritarian government's alternative to American Greenbacks," Gus responds with a cough. He feels miserable, couped-up in this room, restricted by the web that enshrouds him, fatigued by his gunshot wounds. "The Chinese and Russians and the rest of their ilk love *id*. At least it's holding up better than crypto."

Mr. Pootin, playing nurse, dresses Gus's shoulder. The bot's mesh, perhaps due to some special setting, melds with Gus's, allowing the bobblehead to enter the hacker's personal space. The first order of business is dumping medical-grade disinfectant—the motel's complimentary bottle of tequila—onto the ooze near Gus's right clavicle.

"Ouch!" Gus hollers, wincing from the sting. "If you want to pretend to be a licensed medical practitioner operating on me—ya evil puppet—at least use a search engine in that nickel-plated cranium of yours … and learn how to do it *right!*"

Gus tries, and fails, to bite the bot.

"You con-tin-yoo to underestimate me, Henrik Gustavo," Mr. Pootin says with surgical precision, swabbing the flesh wound with a wad of rolled-up toilet paper and wrapping it with a torn off shred of pillowcase. "I'll always be by your side and at your service, making sure … vhat do you Americans say? *You're still kicking.*"

"How about just making sure I'm not kicking *you!*" Gus shouts, rolling to his side, thrashing head and legs away from the bot and his psychotic meddling—and straining to see what the assassin is staring at outside.

Gus's comment falls on deaf ears.

"Poor Henrik Gustavo," says the bobblehead, clucking his metal tongue, checking Gus's forehead for a temperature. "Your fever must be im-pac-ting your ability to think." The bot turns to the assassin. "How long, Master, until—"

"Waaaaait a minute!" Gus shouts, lurching off the bed in a coughing fit—and thwarted back onto the mattress by the tinsel-like webs. He rolls back toward Mr. Pootin. "You insist I treat you as an equal, but you refer to *him* as 'Master?' Are you crazy?"

"Isn't that obvious?" mumbles the assassin from the window.

"Master finalized my settings for dis mission," says the bobblehead, ignoring both slights, hands massaging pillow instead of Gus's head. "Because of dis, I use da term of endearment dat is most app-rope-ri-ate to my programming."

"Geez, Mr. Pootin, how low can you go, bro?" Gus asks, shaking his head. "We need to find you a bidet so you can wash out your central processing unit, because right now you're talking out of your—"

The assassin slips away from the curtain to type on the laptop. Outside, through the gap between the curtain and window frame, Gus spots a Liberator positioned about two miles away. There is also a circling helicopter and drones. They are surveying the area above fields of agave, the new cash crop of the parched Central Valley.

"They're getting close," the assassin informs his robotic minion. "NAM NUZHNO INITSIIROVAT' PROTSEDURY EKSTRENNOY EVAKUATSII!"

The direct translation to English is beyond Gus's comprehension, but he does recognize the Russian cognates for 'procedure' and 'evacuation' in the master's command. Combined with the fact Mr. Pootin's daggers slide out of his fingers and are pressed against Gus's throat—and that the bot's eyes peer down at Gus like irritated hornets—the message to the hacker, at least, seems clear: It's time for him to get out of Dodge. *Unfortunately for you, my dear autocratic enablers, I won't be complying with any further requests.*

It's a new world of no order.

To regroup campers without triggering them, Myles and José decide on a novel approach to host a town hall meeting. First, they rummage the costume shed near the amphitheater. There they obtain props for the performance they plan to provide. Next, they head to the administrative offices—a cluster of abandoned cubicles wedged between the health office and staff cabins—sifting through desk drawers until they find enough batteries to activate the public announcement system. Finally, they broadcast their pitch.

"Greetings, Friendly Foresters," José says, combing his hand through his mullet as he attempts to rally the refugees from the clutches of the apocalypse. "We hope you enjoyed your free time following recent events, but now we would like to come together as a community and figure out what we are going to do next. Please join us in the dining hall for a meeting." Now, the hook. "Anyone who attends will have a chance to share how they're feeling and receive an ice cream cone."

José disconnects and glances at Myles. "How did that sound?"

Myles shrugs. "We'll find out."

Fortunately, the classic strategy—enticing youth to participate with treats—works. Entering the dining hall, a selection of oldies plays in the background, thanks to a dusty record player and electricity provided by the kitchen generator. Arrivals form a line, greeted by Myles and José wearing white aprons and black bowties, soda-shop uniforms from the 1950s. They man their positions behind the serving counter, bopping to the beat of a bygone era while doling out the last batch of chocolate, mint, and vanilla ice cream from the freezer. The two counselors plop scoops onto cones for everyone who appears before them, a hot and bothered rabble following a day of running wild after a nuclear strike.

Judging by the grins, the youngest campers appreciate the cold sweetness. Then again, they tend to be the easiest to please. They still don't fully comprehend what has happened: SoCal is obliterated, and millions are dead. The real proof of the ice cream's effectiveness is the standoffish adolescents, who grudgingly accept their cones without grumbling. A few of them, like Tony, reflect the decency of the past and express gratitude to Myles and José for attempting to ease their worries and boost morale.

"Thank you, Mr. Rodriguez and Mr. Harper," Tony says, licking his mint cone. "You two always find a way to make the rest of us feel at home."

Myles and José nod, savoring the praise. A distracted camper darts past them and slips, causing her vanilla ice cream to splatter on the floor.

After Myles and José mop up the spill, they marvel at the gathering. These youngsters, set loose for a day, are quick to resume the routines of civilization once given the opportunity to lick their wounds, so to speak. *This incredible loss we're experiencing, we're experiencing together*, Myles realizes. Between the infusion of music and sugar, the cafeteria thumps with old-fashioned human energy, camaraderie, and connection. *Hell, maybe tonight we'll light a bonfire, roast marshmallows, and celebrate the lives of the loved ones we've lost …*

"Well-played, fellas," Tiffany says, last of their customers. "I'll have a scoop of chocolate, please."

After the fallout from the fight, this is José's first shot at peace.

"Just in time," he says, scraping the bottom of the tub for the last delicious bits, piling them into a single scoop for his crush. He hands her the cone. "The last spoonful of happiness, for you. Friends?"

Tiffany ignores his question, reaching for the cone.

"Not so fast," José says, pulling away.

"Of course, we're friends, José!" Tiffany bursts. "Even though I would have preferred it if you handled the situation with Geo differently, I admit, your outdated Cro-Magnon Man approach to sticking up for me does show that, at least in your own barbaric way, you respect me." She coughs. "And, of course, my virtue."

"Of course … I do," José says, eyes wet with emotion. "What can I say, girl? You light my fire!"

"Okay," Tiffany says, raising her hands. "Let's not ring the wedding bells yet."

"Right," José says with a smirk, extending his hand, correcting himself. "What I meant to say is, *thank you*."

Tiffany gazes at the outstretched hand.

"No, thank *you*," she says, leaning over the counter, embracing José. Myles notices a tear slip from her eye as she whispers, "*No one* has ever stood up for me like that before. Not even my own father."

"You don't need to be so strong," he says, holding her tight.

"Neither do you," she says, breaking away, wiping the tear from her eye. "Get in here, Myles!"

Myles joins them in the group hug, and by the time they are finished, the cafeteria mirth settles to a mumble. One of the expats, Matt, pulls the record from the player and shuts off the music.

"Are we ready to talk … to the rest of the camp?" Myles asks, his voice faltering as eyes across the dining hall land on him.

"I don't know, Myles, *are you*?" Tiffany prods. She clasps his hand, and together he, she, and José gather at the front of the cafeteria. The last conversations dissolve.

Scott hands Myles a mike.

One of the counselors, sitting in the back, shouts, "What's the word, Mr. Harper? Are we going to use ninja stars to kill the *Kiaskis*?"

A round of laughter.

"I'm thinking it's time to try the tomahawks."

Myles tosses an imaginary one at the commenter, but no one laughs. That's when it hits him: right now, campers aren't looking for a clown. These kids no longer need fun and games. They need leaders to organize the chaos.

"Don't bother trying to win them over, Myles," says a voice from the back of the cafeteria. "In a day, we'll all be dead."

Rows of heads turn to meet the gaze of Geo, eyes partially hidden under the shadow of his sombrero. He stands just outside the open double doors of the dining hall, his feet shoulder width apart, his stomach protruding slightly from a build-up of gassy bravado as he nurses the final the drops of tequila.

"I hope you're wrong," Myles says with a strained voice.

"What's that, man?" Geo asks, hand over ear. Myles realizes it's not a taunt; he really is having difficulty hearing. Myles tugs on José's shoulder, holding back his friend as he takes a step forward, fists clenched.

"Looks like you've organized quite a posse," Geo says, eyes darting across the cafeteria, his mind, like some wild beast, already lost, bouncing from person to person, from one drunken thought to another. He stares at Tiffany. "I'm sorry, but not surprised, to see some staff members who have decided to join you."

"What about you?" Tiffany demands, stepping toward him. "Will *you* join us?"

"Yeah, Geo, why don't you come inside and take a load off?" Myles asks. The support from his peers helps to restore the certainty of his voice. "There's no reason why you need to face what's out there alone."

Instead of luring Geo inside, Myles's comment seems to provoke him. The disgraced counselor takes his last swig of tequila.

"See, that's where you're wrong!" he shouts, pointing at Myles accusatorily. "I've never really been part of the herd, or even a true shepherd of a herd, like you and your cutesy friends passing out your scoops of ice cream. You see, I've always been a wolf in sheep's clothing, and *I've always been alone.*"

"That's not true!" shouts a voice from the crowd. Myles recognizes the little girl with the patch over her eye, bikini top, and shorts. Kylie clambers on top of a table with her bare feet, pointing a tomahawk at Geo. "You're the reason I love this camp!" she exclaims, her grip on the handle loosening with an outpouring of regret. "You played the guitar and sang, and you made me feel free as air every time I saw you! I don't know what happened to make you so angry, Geo, but I want my camp director back!"

"Me, too!" another camper yells.

"Yeah!" shouts another.

Geo takes a step back, absorbing the outcry, his cheeks warming in a way that has nothing to do with the booze he drank.

"There's that smile," Myles says. Geo's grin grows wider and larger, showing off his pearly white teeth. It's at this moment—baring his incisors for all to see—that his body is removed from view by a flash of black.

José screams, "*Kiaski* attack!"

Metal thunder from a helicopter pounds Myles's ears, followed by relentless gunfire. Heads duck under tables as Myles's legs, paralyzingly slow to respond to his mind, leave him marooned in an anxiety-filled pool of quicksand. Suddenly, he's stuck, like in one of his nightmares, struggling to slog forward.

Move!

And just like that, by sheer will, Myles skims past an aisle of tables to the cafeteria's open doors as if he just pressed fast forward in a video game. Outside, he stands where Geo previously stood. A flurry of bullets fly past, and a series of blasts rock the forest south of camp. Myles's jostled gaze shifts from burning trees in the distance to more pressing matters: a trail of blood leads from his feet … to an abandoned sombrero languishing in the dirt … to a crumbled cabin fifty feet away … where he sees Geo … or what's left of him. Dismembered arms and legs are scattered among a pulverized wall.

As Myles surveys the splattered debris, a sleek, dark creature emerges from the rubble. It's larger, but leaner, than the bear he encountered under the stars, and behind the beast rests the gnawed face, chewed eyes, and lifeless grin of the former camp director. Geo's head rolls off its bony torso and falls to the ground with a pitiful thud near the razor-sharp toes of the four-legged monster. A moment since Myles last saw him, Friendly Forest's embattled leader has become a devoured mess.

As the *Kiaski* turns toward Myles, he takes a step back, startled by its hideousness. A cluster of crimson eyes—dozens of glossy, marble-like pupils—brighten before him, illuminated by the blood of a fresh kill. The pupils meander until they hone on the young counselor. The mouth, with a dislocating jaw, drops several inches to reveal rows of jagged teeth that resemble steak knives. Even from this distance, the stench of the bile-colored drool dripping off the monster's spotted tongue makes Myles sick.

Meanwhile, the deafening sound of the helicopter refuses to relent. The *Kiaski* is pelted by a barrage of gunfire, and it recoils, staggering backward from the onslaught of hypersonic metal. The creature's feathery fur must have the consistency of tar, or Kevlar, because bullets bounce off the beast's protective, outer layer. A few manage to penetrate, however, enough for the alpha alien to raise its horned head toward the flaming sun and howl with an out-of-this-world pitch, "BZYR-NIEN-NEEE-BZYR-BIZZRY!"

The sonic overload—like a saber-toothed tiger slamming against the keys of a grand piano—is only buffeted by the whoosh of the rotating helicopter blades. A soldier, positioned behind the chopper's gatling gun, runs out of ammo, and as the empty chamber rotates uselessly, Myles feels overwhelmed with dread: *Reload, reload … reload!*

As if there will ever be enough bullets in this world to nail these flesh-eating beasts into the coffin they deserve.

The soldier barks an order at the pilot as the *Kiaski* snarls, lunging from the cabin rubble to the roof of the dining hall and onto the chopper, clinging to the rail of the aerial machine. The soldier pulls a dagger from her vest as the helicopter twirls in the air. She reaches down toward the monster's head as its claws hook into her thigh. In a single flinging motion, she is airborne and diced in the propeller. Blood, flesh, and guts shower Myles as he watches from the ground.

The *Kiaski's* unexpected weight—or perhaps the soldier's violent death—throws off the pilot. Myles knows he should run for cover, but he can't, mesmerized as the deafening chopper spirals out of control and into the *Command Center*. A ball of flame lights up the smoke-filled sunset, and for a moment, the surrounding redwoods appear like silhouetted gods gazing down at the spectacular damage caused by the cosmic clash.

From the fire, the *Kiaski* appears. Its smoldering fur bursts into flames, a combustible exterior, perhaps, not quite meant for this world. *Maybe you are made of tar; good, then burn!* The hellish hound regards Myles briefly before hobbling into the redwood groves and slipping into the encroaching darkness.

Sweaty palms clasp Myles's hands. Tiffany and José stand at his sides. Behind him, he feels the curious presence of the rest of camp, a community brought together to witness the beginning of their demise. The folks at Friendly Forest stare at the blazing *Command Center*. Myles thinks it used to be called the *Chill Room*, a reference to a life of leisure that no longer exists, but he can't remember for sure. The world is changing too fast for his mind to keep up, and now the building and Jeanie and any connection that they might have offered beyond the present is lost. Like some pre-historic figure ravaged by nature, all Myles manages to do is point at the wreckage and say, "Fire."

Chapter 15

When the assassin opens the motel room door, carrying Alice away in his arms, Gus begins his campaign to undermine Mr. Pootin's questionable priorities and programming. Unfortunately, the bobblehead no longer hovers over his face—insisting on providing the hacker with unsolicited caresses and massages—which would have made accessing the bot's assets less difficult. Instead, Mr. Pootin sits on the table across from the bed, keeping one eye on his captive and the other on the laptop, scrolling through the latest Alice gossip on the net.

"Some conspiracy theorists claim Lady Pro-fit invited da aliens to Earth to force da human race to vork together," Mr. Pootin says. His right eye moves away from the laptop, aligns with his left eye, and they both focus on Gus. "According to dis theory, da arrival of da Spectacle—as you call it—was not a *pre-dic-shon*, but an *in-vi-tay-shon*."

"Based on what evidence?" Gus barks from his strapped, compromised position on the bed.

"No evi-dance, but perhaps a lo-gical conclusion none-da-less," Mr. Pootin says, his pointy, synthetic brow rising from behind the screen. "Just consider, Henrik Gustavo, how unlikely it is dat a person could accurately guess da *exact time* ven an alien in-vay-shon would take place. Seems far-fetched, doesn't it?"

"Not any more far-fetched than a knee-high bot mouthing off about it," Gus responds. "When did you become such a skeptic? You started off rooting for Alice and the human race, and now your cold, clinical Russian wiring must finally be getting the best of you. Unfortunately, Mr. Pootin, your logic is off."

"How so?" asks the bobblehead, right brow rising higher than the Sierras, peeved by the hacker's critique.

"You claim Alice *cannot* predict the future, but she *can* telepathically communicate with extraterrestrials?" Gus says, pondering the possibilities as he lies on his back and stares at the popcorn ceiling. "One notion makes no more sense than the other, but we have ample evidence that Alice *does* know *when* major events *will* occur, because she *says* they will occur, and they *do*. That's why she's famous, dude. Therefore, I'd say any half-baked 'theory' posted on the net that she invited the aliens to invade Earth is ... garbage."

Slowly, the brow on the bot's forehead lowers to a horizontal level along with his effective filter.

"Dat makes me feel better, Henrik Gustavo," Mr. Pootin says, blinking affectionately. "I prefer to live in a vorld dat has a lit-tell magic and hope. Alice's psychic powers, at least, present dat possibility."

"Great, then put your money where your mouth is, and let me go. We can still save Alice *and* the planet."

"And ignore my prime direct-tif?" Mr. Pootin asks, slamming shut the laptop. "Dat vould be an insult to my Master and da vonderful Kremlin developers hoo created me. How could I do dat to dem?"

Through the crack in the window curtain, Myles sees the assassin open the trunk and dump Alice's unconscious body into the back of the sedan. In the distance, the Liberator remains an unflinching tower, suspiciously immobile, like some pissed-off parent preparing to discipline a misbehaving child.

"You better choose what side you want to be on soon, Mr. Pootin, because the situation is about to get *serious*."

While Atta places Alice in the stolen F.B.I. vehicle, a sub-screen pops open in the bottom corner of the Liberator's cockpit display, revealing three approaching red dots from a satellite radar.

"Incoming mechs," ACE says.

"Are they backup?"

"Negative, commander," responds his computerized co-pilot, relaying the internal dialogue between Daddy's Girl and the approaching mechs. "*Access error. Systems unavailable.* They're bad actors, sir. Central processors jacked. Prepare for a strike."

"How long?"

"One-hundred and eighty miles out. Three minutes."

Inside the cockpit, Ray glances to his right as he reaches behind his back. Outside, to the right of the cockpit shield, the call sign on the Liberator's shoulder, "Mama's Boy #1," stretches as the mech's saginium sheets expand, and the robot's right hand withdraws a saber from a sheath behind its shoulder. As Ray clasps his hands together, the last of the gelatinous material that encapsulates him vaporizes, and the smart threads that weave around his body dissolve into a pulsing efflorescent layer that coats his suit, helmet, and gloves.

"Power-up," ACE says, and Ray's hands tingle with an electricity that surges through the mech into the saber.

From the cockpit display, he sees the mech's hands grip the handle of the huge razor-sharp sword, which ignites with a fiery, laser glow.

"Let's roll, ACE."

"Da Liberator, Master!" shouts the bobblehead, yanking the curtain wide, so the view outside the motel room is clear. He bangs on the window, so the assassin sees the bot calling to him. "It's coming for you!"

Atta ignores the warning and glances down at the psychic, tucked in the fetal position in the trunk of the sedan. He checks her pulse, just to be sure. Alive. At least the ensuing battle will be worth the price. Delivering the young woman to the Russians will pay the assassin enough to retire in leisure and pursue his favorite pastime.

"Alpine skiing, I'm coming for you," he reminds himself.

Atta peeks around the open trunk. His Radical sunglasses, with their augmented lenses, place Mama's Boy #1 at just over three kilometers and closing. The mech, likely piloted by the legendary Ray Salvatore, advances toward the parking lot at a steady gait wielding a bright, laser-sharp sword. Should the trifecta of inbound Liberators that the assassin hacked using a Tr8tor virus fail to outmatch the commander and his A.I. partner, ACE, the plan to ensure Alice Walker arrives at the Kremlin includes other contingencies ...

Atta reaches for the box behind Walker's unconscious body and fumbles through the lock combination like a hapless thief. He must hurry, even if his mission couldn't have been better timed.

As soon as the psychic posted her prediction on Bestagram about an imminent alien invasion, Atta's preparations no longer were a theoretical exercise. Terminating the F.B.I.'s field captain at his home—then impersonating him through a voice-modification program on his laptop as he concealed himself inside the F.B.I. vehicle assigned to monitor Walker— was a successful ploy only because Atta had been surveilling the team of agents for six months, and he was well-positioned to leverage such developments in his favor. He had to be incredibly careful how he approached the psychic; and fate, it turns out, provided him with the perfect opening.

As the North American military establishment scrambled to assess the extraterrestrial threat after a starship crash landed off the Southern California coast, it left the powers-that-be distracted and exposed to more traditional, Earth-bound forms of infiltration. An incredible opportunity presented itself to seize Alice Walker, the West's greatest free-roaming asset, and turn the tide of Earth's destiny toward the East's global leadership. Atta's Russian and Chinese counterparts would be proud.

The box pops open, and Atta withdraws a rocket launcher from the trunk. He steps to the side of the sedan, and with the guidance of his eyewear, he pinpoints his target: a seam one-foot wide that separates the armored plates tucked in the right armpit, beneath the call sign, of the mech's shoulder.

Atta pulls the trigger. A projectile is fired that leaves a trail of smoke as it spirals through the air. From the canister, a drone, the size of a shoe, unfolds. It has a long, penetrating snout and buzzing wings. The mosquito-like machine zigzags on an eyeball-rolling course toward Mama's Boy #1.

"Good luck, Commander Salvatore, swatting that bug," the assassin says with a satisfied grin. He tosses the spent rocket launcher onto the ground, slams the trunk shut, and hops into the driver's seat of the sedan.

In the cockpit, Ray ceases to jog, and the Liberator stops.

For a moment, onlookers like Gus might suspect the tower of tech is bewildered as it scans over fields of agave. Water-demanding almond and citrus groves, the staple crop of the Central Valley for a hundred years, are being replaced in the twenty-first century, hectare by hectare, with endless rows of the drought-tolerant pointy plants, which provide alcohol and nutrients to impoverished locals. However, Mama's Boy #1 is not surveying the changing agricultural landscape. Ray monitors the buzzing drone whirling in the space that separates him from Alice, and the mech adopts a defensive, stationary position as he determines how to proceed.

"It's too low," ACE says. "Any gunfire aimed at the drone will threaten our target. More bad news, sir: Twenty Hellfire missiles inbound from the rogue Liberators."

Ray sighs, resigning himself to receiving the first blows in what he anticipates will be an epic firefight. Within the cockpit, he crouches into a ball, falling into an ergonomic cushion that stabilizes his body. "Discharge countermeasures. Prepare for impact."

"Aye, sir."

Firework-like strands of platinum alloy, part of the Lib's jessinium overlay, burst into the air, creating a magnetic shield around Mama's Boy #1.

"Daddy's Girl is set at maximum force-field protection," ACE says. "Brace yourself, commander."

Ray closes his eyes. The effervescent coat smothering his suit, helmet, and gloves brightens into a wiry lattice that connects his body to countless points around the cockpit. Within this network, the material in the air solidifies, transforming from a gas to a gelatinous substance that crystalizes into a cocoon around the commander. As Ray lies motionless, folded into himself, anticipating the oncoming onslaught, his mind drifts to Sara. He imagines what his daughter is creating in her university-level art class.

"Vait, Master, Vait!" Mr. Pootin cries, shattering the motel room window with a balled fist, tears of black oil streaming from his eyes. "I only vant to serve you! Please! Don't leaf me!"

"Tough break, hey?" Gus says, flopping up and down in the restrictive mesh, trying like an awkward caterpillar to leverage his body into an upright position. He pauses, out of breath, and continues to speak, sitting at the edge of the bed. "Think about how I feel. Your Master promised me a new career, but it was just talk, a trick to ensure I behave. This mission was never about *you*, Mr. Pootin, or *me*. Only *her*. And now he has her, and *she* is gone."

Mr. Pootin slips deeper into the chair, shoulders sunk, head low, the embodiment of boy-toy depression. "Vhat now?"

Gus manages to fidget upright from the mattress, feet planted firmly on the carpet. He gazes with a commanding view at the bobblehead and beyond, through the motel room window of external reality and freedom.

"You want the truth?"

The bobblehead nods. His facial sheets crease, revealing the sad desperation of an abandoned child. "Of course, I vant da truth, Henrik Gustavo! You are all I haf left in dis cruel vorld!"

The bot dashes from the chair, folding his over-sized head into Gus's crotch, smothering his legs with hugs. The hacker resists the urge to kick the psychopathic droid off him. Instead, he caresses his head and assures him, "Now, now, everything is going to be okay ..."

Outside, a series of explosions light up the darkening sky. The Liberator, their rescuer, is nowhere to be seen, covered by a hellish whirlwind of missile fire. Mr. Pootin glances up, following Gus's gaze. The bobblehead grips the extra mesh around Gus's hands, like a frightened kid clinging to the ends of a blanky.

"The truth is, Mr. Pootin, your Master didn't leave us here to be rescued," Gus says. "The first rule of any crime is to get rid of the evidence. He left us here as his final weapon. We're going to die—unless you help me."

"Vhat should I do?" the bobblehead insists, clinging to Gus, unwilling to let go of the mesh.

"Set me free, so I can set you free."

Gus recalls the absurd phrase in Russian related to Putin's decadent palace that is used to restrict the bobblehead. If saying *'akva discoteka'* causes the bot's knives to recede into his hands, saying the phrase in English will free the knives—and the hacker.

"AQUA DISCOTECH!"

Mr. Pootin's blades uncoil from his fingers, slicing through the mesh balled in his hands. Gus tears through the gap in the threads, untangling his arms. The bobblehead watches with wonder, then vexation, as Gus grabs him and plops him on the bed.

"You treat me like child!" Mr. Pootin warns, kicking and screaming as Gus wraps the bot in the sheets. He yanks the twisted end of the rolled-up bedding and tosses the diabolically annoying machine into the closet, a bag of dirty laundry. Gus hops to the closet, braces it shut with one hand while he unfurls himself from the rest of the restrictive mesh with the other. He won't be able to contain the bot for long.

"Henrik Gustavo, *you* betrayed *me!*" Mr. Pootin shouts from inside the closet, using his head as a battering ram to bust through the door.

THUMP!

THUMP!

THUMP!

THUMP!

THUMP!

THUMP!

Each exploding missile feels like a knuckle punch to Ray's head. Thirty knocks, and the head-banging ends. Following the bombardment, the commander wills himself to stand inside Mama's Boy #1. The protective insulation dissolves from a solid to gas, restoring maximum mobility within the cockpit again.

Almost immediately, the commander senses a problem: a hot sting under his right armpit, and white noise bursts into his ears.

"ACE, you here?"

"Barely," sounds the feverish computerized co-pilot. "Drone waited for the bombardment—and our defenses—to fall, then it snuck into our air space and stung me. Quite a bug, sir. Daddy's Girl is upset. Systems struggling to keep a head up."

Through Ray's display, he sees a mosquito-like drone flake off the underarm of the Lib and plunge to the ground below.

"Rogue mechs?"

"Thirty seconds," ACE says.

"Kick me to the curb."

The commander leans back, falling through an expanding hole in the cockpit. He is funneled down the mech's throat in a viscous tube that spirals past the Lib's thorax and its nuclear-fuel heart to the inner workings of the pelvis, firing from the sphincter in a casing that transforms midair into a motorbike that lands Ray gently onto the ground, rocketing him forward between the mech's legs.

Ray, still in his body suit, gazes from his helmet, weaving the motorbike through fields of agave, locking onto the sedan pulling out of the Sierra View parking lot onto a two-lane highway.

"Good luck," ACE says. In Ray's helmet, he hears a whoosh of wind created by the arriving Liberators.

The battle begins.

"You, too."

As Gus holds the closet door shut and contemplates how to keep the bobblehead as far away from himself as possible, he hears the roar of clashing Liberators raging in the distance. He glances outside the window, and like some childhood fever dream, he gazes in amazement at the flailing arms and legs as four mechs rumble.

Man, I gotta get a closer look at this …

That's when an idea seizes him, a way to keep Mr. Pootin out of his personal space forever. *It's time to let go.* Amid the bobblehead's thumping and whining, Gus releases the knob, tiptoes to the front door, opens it wide—and dashes into the bathroom. He sits on the toilet, contemplating his fate in semi-darkness. Will the bobblehead fall for the bait, pursue him outside, and get distracted by the mech brawl? Gus realizes he is banking on a lot, including that the bot really is as much of a boy as he seems.

Eventually, Mr. Pootin ceases his head banging, realizes he's spouting off inside an echo chamber, and quietly turns the knob. Gus hears the jangle of the bot's metal mesh drop to the floor, and from the door crack, he sees the shadow of tiny feet scamper from the closet. The springs of the mattress squeak as the bot bounces on the bed, free and unfettered from any human oversight.

"Vee!" Mr. Pootin shouts, indulging in a round of juvenile gymnastics. "Veeeee!"

Like an inspired sous chef, the bobblehead's knuckle-knives slice through the bed's pillows, causing the motel room to snow countless white feathers that litter the dirt-stained carpet.

"Where'd you go, Henrik Gustavo?" beckons the killer bot. The knives cut through the motel room walls, sending shards of plaster tumbling onto the floor. "Playing hide-and-seek, my friend?"

Gus wants to protest, tell Mr. Pootin he's tired of their toxic relationship, that friends don't let friends get mixed up with world-class assassins, but he does not fall for the trick. The bot is already lost, his allegiances hard-wired into his mainframe. The hacker wants to live, so he keeps his mouth shut.

As if reading Gus's thoughts, the sentient machine's eyes rest on the bathroom, and the hacker protectively pulls up his feet, squatting on the toilet seat with arms wrapped around legs. Making his final stand on the potty, he realizes, may not have been the smartest idea. Surely the bobblehead can bio-scan behind the walls and register where he is, crouched on the crapper, desperate to be invisible.

However, the bot's wires must be profoundly crossed because Gus's location does not seem to compute. He hears the knives, languishing in the walls, withdraw.

"Vee!" Mr. Pootin shrieks, followed by the squeaky springs of the mattress as the bobblehead bounces off bed, onto floor, and out the front door. "I can't vait to find you, Henrik Gustavo!" he says, voice fading into the combative clash of the distant Liberators. "Today, ve shall play... *ruff*. You ... hear ... me, Henrik Gustavo? *Ruffffff!*"

Silence.

Gus steps off the toilet and breathes. The relief to his mind is immediate, like stepping off a roller coaster he's been riding for months. Mr. Pootin is gone.

Ray clears the agaves on the motorbike and accelerates on a two-lane highway toward the Sierra View Motel.

"ACE, I'm not getting reception," he says, topping off on the highway at one-hundred-and-fifty miles per hour. "Your bug is bugging me, too. Any readings from the inn? Good place for an ambush."

"Daddy's Girl is down," ACE says, voice sounding like a can of soda gone flat. "The system infiltration is worse than I thought, sir. Mama's Boy #1 is running off old algorithms right now."

"Copy."

That's when Ray notices the tiny, boy-like creature with an over-sized head darting from the motel parking lot toward the motorbike, waving his arms in exaggerated surrender. Ray's helmet zooms in on the face of the famous, dissatisfied dictator, his eyes lighting up like fiery coals.

It's not surrendering, Ray thinks. *It's on a suicide mission.*

The commander veers left, the opposite side of the highway, pulling away from the orphaned bot's seething rage.

Atta glances in the rearview mirror, enjoying the view. His Radicals confirm it is Ray Salvatore approaching from the south on the motorbike as his struggling Liberator is kicked around by the rogue mechs.

"Don't worry, commander," he says to himself. "Death is coming for you, too."

The Radicals track Ray Salvatore's location in relation to the blast range of the bobblehead's detonating device, and as the sedan hauls away Alice, the assassin counts out loud in Russian, *"A-deen, dva, tree ..."*

Staring out the room's window, Gus is amazed at what he sees. An impaired black Liberator, Mama's Boy #1, swaggers back and forth, moaning, groaning, and barely able to stand as it is pommeled by three patriot-issue mechs painted red, white, and blue. The dust and noise caused by the brutal fight is a distraction from the pathetic plight immediately before him: Mr. Pootin in the parking lot, waving arms hysterically, flagging down a motorbike zipping toward the Sierra View Motel.

As the motorbike swerves around the bobblehead, Gus realizes the bot isn't begging to be rescued, and a tear trickles down his eye as he takes cover.

"Goodbye, my frenemy."

Inside the F.B.I.'s sedan, Atta utters a command, his Radicals send the signal, and he grins as he gazes though the sedan's rearview mirror.

Gus braces himself under the table as the blast from exploding Mr.

Pootin rips through the motel.

Ray's motorbike, with its armor alloy, sustains minor damage from the explosion and continues to rocket toward its target. Ray is not so lucky, however, sustaining a gash in his right femur where a piece of debris—a lone finger-turned-knife—has sliced through his suit and burrowed itself in his thigh.

"How are you holding up, ACE?"

"I've … seen … better … days," says the Lib's sentient co-pilot, communication interrupted by the mechs' powerful blows.

"Help is coming," Ray says.

"You, help me?" ACE says sarcastically. "Now there's a change."

"All can't be lost yet," Ray says. "You still have a sense of humor."

The sound of metal on metal. ACE screams through the com-link.

"Not for long, I fear."

Ray, on the other hand, is feeling better thanks to his body suit. The tattered area around his femur contracts, preventing blood loss. Oozing onto the flesh wound from the frayed material is an antibiotic and sedative that helps to stabilize the leg and allows the commander to ignore the pain of the injury, so he can continue to focus on the task at hand.

The motorbike accelerates, reaching the left side of the sedan. Atta fires several rounds from his revolver, which deflect off Ray's ride, but a bullet grazes his Kevlar-protected suit and stings his right elbow.

Atta swerves toward the motorbike. Ray dodges him. As the commander realigns with the sedan, he flips a switch, and a barrel extends from the right side of the motorbike.

"Come on, baby, light my fire," the commander says, and a tiny laser, barely visible to the naked eye, slices into the midsection of the vehicle.

Ray leans the motorbike right, down toward the ground, then left up toward the sky, creating enough latitude to increase the girth of the incision. Atta slows the sedan, hoping to better align his gun with Ray's head, but it's too late.

The sedan splits in half. Atta and the dislodged front section of the sedan skid and veer off the highway.

Ray's motorbike slows and transforms into a mini-mech that encapsulates his body. He walks in the robotic frame toward the trunk of the severed vehicle, punches a hole in it, reaches inside, and pops it open. Therein lies Alice Walker, a mysterious individual he's only seen in-person twice.

Ten years grown since he last set eyes on her, she's now a woman, lying unconscious in the trunk of the sedan in her classic red hoodie, practically a superhero costume. She remains beautifully stoic, breathing gently, golden wisps of wavy hair covering closed eyes, her pupils oscillating beneath their lids as she dwells in an R.E.M slumber. The national security risk, as well as national treasure, always finds a way to help North America remain free, Ray realizes, despite the danger that often comes with such personal sacrifice.

What could she be dreaming?

Ray steps away from the trunk, scans the highway, and identifies the front section of the split-apart sedan, off the shoulder one-hundred feet ahead. His mini-mech's bio readings detect no sign of Herio Atta.

"The assassin slipped away," he says into this com-link.

"I'm sorry to hear that, sir," ACE says, groaning, "but I'm also envious. I wish I could escape the predicament I'm in."

"And now, you will," Ray says, establishing remote control over Mama's Boy #1. "It's time we send the heaps of metal ganging up on you back to the junkyard where they belong. When you wake, my friend, you'll be free of bugs. Promise."

"Thank you, sir," the co-pilot says with a sigh, relinquishing Daddy's Girl to the commander.

Ray virtually positions himself inside the Liberator's cockpit. The advantage that *Homo Sapiens* have over machines is that humans, at their base, remain an unpredictable species. Standing on the highway, the commander in his mini-mech throws punches, kicks, and fakes that Mama's Boy #1 mirrors in the distance. The rogue machines struggle to adjust to Ray's peculiar combination of karate, gymnastics, and vaudeville theatrics, and the Liberator quickly overtakes its assailants.

After the blast, Gus cautiously stands.

It's like a party that got way out of hand. The window of the motel room is shattered, and glimmering bits of shrapnel litter the walls. Pieces of smoldering debris from the blast mix with feathers from shredded pillows and cover the carpet, leaving the floor to slowly simmer. Even Gus's ears feel like they've been blown out by a set of concert-sized speakers.

The ringing starts to subside as he steps outside. The only remains of Mr. Pootin are his head, which Gus finds wedged under a rear tire of a parked pickup truck. He lifts the mangled face off the ground and regards it in his hands. Even now, in this compromised state, he marvels at the deceased droid's mischievous countenance.

At first, Gus mistakes the grumbling in the distance for thunder. He glances up and watches with youthful glee as Mama's Boy #1, underdog no more, is possessed by the vengeful spirit of a super soldier. The Liberator taunts and tortures with laughable ease the rogue mechs that attempt to gang up and destroy it.

A juke to the right, followed by a swing kick, and the head of a mesmerized enemy sails through the air like a soccer ball. A backflip toward the sky, and a hard dive back to Earth with a firing jetpack and raised laser sword leads to an enemy dismembered from neck to knee.

Man, I wish I had popcorn …

Chapter 16

As the tandem-rotor Chinook touches down at the Sierra View Motel parking lot, Henrik Gustavo has a strong premonition that his adventurous pairing with the psychic is doomed to continue.

"Greetings, Gus," says the voice of a no-nonsense man the hacker immediately recognizes. The fugitive turns and finds a mini-mech facing him. The helmet visor rises, revealing a set of grayish, hawk-like eyes.

"Ray Salvatore?"

"I see you haven't lost your ability to find trouble," the commander says.

"No ... sir," Gus responds, gazing at unconscious Alice draped over the mini-mech arms. "I see you are still ... saving lives?"

"The important ones, at least," the commander says, glancing at the helicopter on standby. "I'm sure you've been through quite an ordeal, Gus, but I need your help."

"As you probably know, I usually don't play nice with government types," says the gun-shy computer wiz, "but you saved my life once, so I guess I owe you one."

"If you give me the intel I need, you will be pardoned by the NAITFSD."

"The … huh?"

"The North American Intergovernmental … my employer," Ray says, giving up explaining the acronym. He foists Alice over his steel shoulder and marches up the ramp of the aerial transport. "Don't you read the headlines, genius? Times are changing. So is our nation's government."

"Suuuuure … *where* are you taking us?" Gus hollers over the thundering propellers, following Ray. Inside the cabin, the commander hands Alice to a team of medics, who place her on a gurney, and he waits for the ramp to close behind Gus, sealed inside the Chinook, before he responds.

"We're heading to your old stomping ground," Ray says, "where your story with Alice began."

"And you saved my life," Gus says, the air for the words barely escaping his lungs. "Paranormal Plantation."

As the helicopter crash ignites a blustery inferno, Myles watches for what feels like eternity, staring at the spire of flames that dance tauntingly before him. With the downed aircraft, he realizes it's too late: for Jeanie, the director of Camp Friendly Forest buried inside the burning *Command Center*; for the pilot and soldier killed in the chopper now serving as the fire's kindling; for Geo, the controversial counselor turned into bits; and Myles's own deceased family and millions of others terrorized by the aliens. With such knowledge, he cannot help but feel slighted by the universe. Humanity's impending doom might be its story, *for now*, but he refuses to believe such annihilation must be its story *forever*. The *Kiaskis* deserve payback for the destruction they've caused, and the displaced Angeleno intends to give it to them. Rage burns through his veins, a fuel as combustible as the blaze before him. Standing transformed by his hate, questioning the tragic absurdity of his species' first contact with a horrific extraterrestrial race, he hears a feminine voice.

Mind your escape.

"What?"

No response from the void, and the voice fades along the telepathic wind in which it arrived.

Myles's mouth feels detached from his brain.

"What … wat … water," he utters, pointing like a caveman at the flames. "Fight … fire … with water!"

"Thanks for the update, Captain Obvious," Tiffany says, her knuckles nudging Myles. "Can someone check on the horses?"

"I will," José says, disappearing in the darkness toward the sound of their anxious neighing.

Myles gazes down and sees that Tiffany is passing him a bucket. He hands the sloshing bucket to Scott, who passes it to Richard, who passes it to Matt, who passes it to Kylie, the little girl in the bikini top with the pirate patch over her eye, and the only one present dressed for an apocalypse. The chain of familiar faces ends with Tony, his tiny muscles popping out of a USC Trojans T-shirt as he grabs the bucket with both hands and hurls the water onto the flames. Loud sparks and smokey resistance follow, and a turf war between campers and conflagration begins.

"More," Myles says—or thinks he says—because try as he may to avoid the seductive allure of the flames, he feels his eyes waver, overcome with fatigue, or is it simply despair? Fortunately, his peers are in sync with this organized activity, and the line of liquid-filled buckets continues to arrive faithfully from the cafeteria, forcing Myles to remain awake and respond to the task at hand.

Sweat drips from the collectively flushed faces until the heat from the flames finally abates. By dawn, there is only a charred, unrecognizable heap of ash and debris left in a smoldering ruin.

"Well done, lads," Scott says.

Myles wanders the wreckage and confirms the fire is dead. "It's time for a break."

Although the rescue effort does not spare the *Commander Center*, the counselors and campers of Friendly Forest have prevented the blaze from spreading to surrounding cabins—a good thing, since all anyone wants after the ordeal is to crash in their bunks and sleep off their terror. The problem is that may not be a good idea. As the expats lead campers back to their beds, Myles returns the buckets to the cafeteria. Inside, he finds approximately one-third of the camp's staff and children where he last saw them. Seated across the dining hall, separated by the empty spaces of those who moved on, the eyes of these 'sleepers' oscillate beneath their lids, trickles of vomit staining their lips.

"What happened to them?"

"The same thing that happened to Jeanie," José says, yanking off his soda-shop bowtie and grimy apron. "The *Kiaskis* got the best of them. They've been scared to death."

"That's the problem," Tiffany says, snapping her fingers in front of an unconscious girl. "They're *not* dead. Still breathing."

"Not quite alive, though, so what exactly *are* they?" José wonders as he regards the comatose male camper propped up next to him. "I don't get it. If it's a choice between being eaten alive by a *Kiaski* or drifting off to oblivion, I'd rather die fighting and take one of those nasty-ass beasts with me."

"Despite all of the rejection you've faced this summer," Tiffany says with a smirk, "it's nice to see you haven't lost your mojo."

José rolls his eyes. "Just sayin,' we gotta kill these damn space dogs, before they kill us."

"How?" Myles asks.

"Friendly Forest would have burned down if it weren't for the group effort putting out the flames," Tiffany says. "I don't know how to rid us of aliens, but I do know our only hope for surviving is working together."

"Maybe, but working together is *exhausting*," José says, stretching his arms. "Man, I'm beat."

"Me, too," Tiffany says.

"Me, three," Myles says, interjecting himself at the table between them. He takes a seat.

"What do we tell the kids?" José asks. "Is it safe to fall asleep?"

"Are you afraid that if you fall asleep, you'll never wake up?" Tiffany asks, leaning on Myles's shoulder.

"Pretty much," José says, also leaning on Myles's shoulder.

"Then fear already won," Myles says, eyes fluttering. "There's no point in staying awake."

"I'm not ready to die," José says, closing his eyes. "My mind and body just need to rest."

"I agree," Tiffany mumbles with a yawn. "We'll think a little clearer after we catch some z's."

Myles feels the weight of his friends as they collapse into unconsciousness, and he becomes shrouded in a veil of darkness.

Illuminated by the consciousness-expanding light, the Chinook travels by night along the northern perimeter of the Spectacle. Strapped in their seats, commander situated across from fugitive, they watch between them as the medical staff tend to Alice. The blinding extraterrestrial glow, an assault on their senses, shines through the chopper's windows.

"Sleep," the commander says as the shutters close. "The ordeal you've been through is nothing compared to what's coming. I'll need you fresh in the morning."

It's an order Gus graciously accepts. Over the Sierras they go, and as they do so, the hacker dreams of freedom. He is back in Oakland, leaving Veggie Terri Ann's after breakfast. This time he strolls out of the establishment not with Alice, but alone, grateful and satisfied. Roaming the city's streets, he meets a woman with short hair in a flowered dress, nursing a slushie and walking a Labrador. Gus falls for her and her dog instantly. He proposes to her there on the sidewalk.

Despite his noblest of intentions, the engagement feels awkward and rushed. As he professes his eternal love to the woman, she spills her slushie, and he wanders off on a quest to find her a napkin to clean up the mess.

He stumbles into a gun store. The shelves are lined with weapons— light sabers, rocket packs, ray guns—tech that, despite their popularity in science fiction, do not quite belong on 2036 Earth.

Sort of like Liberators.

"Can I help you?" asks an old lady with stained teeth sipping coffee behind the checkout counter.

"I need a napkin."

"You can find anything you want *there*," she says, pointing beyond the store's otherworldly merchandise to a backroom pulsating with an ominous glow. Too afraid to move, Gus sees walls lined with countless black eyes dripping tears of gooey slime. When he glances back at the old lady, a third eye opens along the crease of her forehead. The eye is blacker than the coffee in the mug, and it stares at Gus.

He startles awake.

"Bad dream?" the commander asks.

"It didn't feel like a dream," Gus says. He gazes at Alice in the gurney, so serene, except for her pupils, shifting back and forth maniacally beneath their lids. What does she have in store for them next? "It felt like a world ... just beyond our own."

The Chinook's shutters open. For a moment, the Spectacle remains out of sight, behind them, and the commander and fugitive are met by a spoke-wheel sunrise gleaming to the east over the sands of the Mojave. The helicopter whips around in a circle, and as it descends, the Institute comes into view. The white monstrosity resembles an Antebellum-style mansion. Supported by sunbaked pillars and an architectural tradition tied to slavery, the majestic edifice creates an illusion of civilization as it rises from a high-desert wasteland.

Returning to this awful place feels like visiting a haunted house where memories refuse to die. The mysterious building, once considered a refuge for renegade scientists, was established in the early twentieth century as part of California's eugenics program. After serving as a ghastly site for neurological experiments conducted on the deformed and disabled, the Institute's staff expanded their research during the Cold War to investigate a wider array of mental activity ranging from enhanced spy techniques to telepathy. The tradition of exploring fringe fields of science continued into the last decade with the era of the super kids—juvenile delinquents, orphans, and other gifted children, such as Alice and Gus, forcibly removed from their homes or taken off the streets to serve as lab rats for various psychological studies.

"Who runs Paranormal Plantation now?" Gus asks as the Chinook touches down in a dirt clearing.

"The *Institute* is managed by the N-A-I ..." the commander starts to rattle off the acronym and cuts himself short. "My employer has an agreement with California's Eco-Socialists, who took over the site shortly after your release."

The commander seems less guarded and more conversational, Gus notices, after changing into field fatigues during their flight. His mech, now a motorbike, is propped against a chair next to him.

Ray's casual demeanor inspires the hacker to be blunt.

"It wasn't a 'release,' sir," he explains. "It was a *liberation*. Our internment was worse than what the Feds did to the Japanese during World War II."

"Are you referring to Manzanar?" Ray asks, pointing out his window. "That's only twenty miles north—"

"I know where it is," Gus says, "and Area 51 is only one hundred miles that way," he adds, pointing out his window, "but I'm not talking about sightseeing, commander. A lot of us have scars from our experience at the Institute."

They watch as Alice is unloaded from the Chinook.

"That's quite a comparison," Ray says, unstrapping his harness, following medical team down the ramp. "The folks interned at Manzanar had their property seized, whole families stripped of their rights, dignity, freedom, and wealth. On the other hand, you and your friends enjoyed first-class treatment at the government's top-notch facility. You were like kids at summer camp, really."

"A camp none of us volunteered to attend!" Gus shouts, unstrapping his harness, following Ray down the ramp. "You know it wasn't right."

"Fine," the commander concedes, and he changes course as they disembark from the chopper, cutting toward Paranormal Plantation.

It's a pleasant morning—still below a hundred degrees—and the shadow of the white-washed mansion towers over them like a peculiar roadside attraction en route to Las Vegas. "I'm just glad I arrived when I did, to lead the evacuation."

"*Evacuation*," Gus says, mulling over the word play. "I guess that's the closest I'm ever going to get to an apology from the government."

Ray does not respond. They march up the front steps of the foreboding research facility. Much of it appears as the hacker remembers, minus the wear and tear caused by time and neglect. A layer of sandy crud, formed from the relentless downwind weather of the Sierras, cakes the exterior walls. In the past, exotic plants and lush foliage from around the world lined the building, making the Institute appear at least as much a Garden of Eden as it was a sanctuary for madness.

Today, signs of vegetative life are mostly gone, except for occasional weeds poking up through cracks in walkways. The front foyer, however, remains intact, including its fountain, which continues to operate in grand absurdity. Surrounded by a few overgrown shrubs is a statue of a man with a walrus mustache dressed in an early twentieth-century suit. One hand is raised in greeting as they enter the great hall, the other shoved below his waist, presumably to hold his penis in place. A spout of water arcs from his pelvis, over the bushes, and into a pond filled with stinky muck.

"Professor Jerome B. Goode," Gus says, pausing to share his disdain for the old bust. "A trip to Paranormal Plantation would be incomplete without stopping to appreciate its founding father as he pisses on nature."

Ray confirms the statue depicts the famous eugenicist, who became disillusioned after Hitler lost World War II and forfeited the possibility of 'purifying' the human race. During the Cold War that followed, as America became less fearful of fascists and more fearful of communists, Professor Jerome B. Goode saw an opportunity to make a mark on history. He bought the site from the state of California and bequeathed it to the federal government to help fight the spread of Marxism.

"The Institute became a top-notch center for paranormal research, a purpose it served well until it was shuttered by the Eco-Socialists a few years ago," Ray says, gazing at the fountain sculpture. "At least something still works around here, even it's just a memorial to a crazy old man."

A call comes in on the commander's walkie-talkie. He listens, responds "affirmative," and turns to Gus. "I need you to get this place back online for a scientific team that is on the way. We need to figure out what this anomaly is … and what the status of Southern California is."

"How can I help?"

"Water is running, but the main generators are down," he says. "Once we get them going, the medical lab will need software updates."

"Yes … sir, but are you sure about … me?" Gus asks. "The last time someone offered me a job—yesterday—they changed their mind and tried to blow me up with a bobblehead that looked like Vladmir Putin."

"Funny, but if the Russians are your enemy, then maybe we have more in common than you think," the commander says. He takes one last look at the statue of Professor Jerome B. Goode and directs his attention toward the young man. "Besides, Alice wrote in her notebook that it's okay to 'TRUST GUS.'"

"Really?" Gus asks, trying to suppress his amusement. "Well, in that case, sir, I'm glad to hear we're both on the same page."

Chapter 17

The aroma of bacon and eggs sizzling in a pan, combined with a body odor that smells of sweaty onions, rouses Myles awake with a sensation that lies somewhere between hunger and nausea.

"Oh, my," he gasps, removing his nose from José's armpit, tossing his buddy's arm off his head. "*That* is a nightmare I never want to wake to again."

Tiffany, freshly changed into a clean Friendly Forest T-shirt and blue jeans, emerges from the cafeteria kitchen with two glasses of orange juice.

"I woke up from you snoring," she says. "I was curled up by myself at the edge of the table, while you two lovebirds were as snug as can be."

"A short-lived bromance," José says, stretching. "Is that breakfast I smell, or Myles's dirty hair?"

Tiffany hands the guys their orange juice and returns to the kitchen. Myles sips his drink and contemplates the unconscious children scattered around the cafeteria. They sit and stand, eyes closed, mannequins preserved in the act of drinking, resting, or turning, as if listening to a nearby stranger, some phantom figure whispering in their ear and causing such debilitating terror that they parted ways from the living. Lulled into this trance, with only their fleshy selves that remain, it's as if they are waiting to be harvested by the *Kiaskis*, fuel for the monsters' insatiable desire for flesh.

Perhaps it is better to be in a spell when the moment arrives than to be awake while you are eaten alive.

In a way, Myles is envious. He wants to talk about the strange condition of his peers, but what's the point? He and his friends are still tethered to a reality in which they have a choice: fade or fight.

He glances at José, watching him. They read each other's faces, seem to share the same thought.

"Rest—in our case, anyway—seems to have done us some good," Myles says. "I guess we're still lucky to be alive."

"Guess so," José says.

Glancing out the cafeteria door, Myles tries to gauge the time, based on the length and position of trees' shadows, but his senses are off. "How long did we sleep?"

"Most of the day," Tiffany says, returning from the kitchen with three plates of food stacked on one arm and carrying a carafe of coffee, cups, forks, and napkins. "The sun should be setting in a few hours."

"Dang," José says, marveling at the spread: bacon, eggs, potatoes, toast, and enough caffeine to jumpstart an alien resistance. "You're quite a hostess. Only *mi abuela* does better. You sure you're not Mexican?"

"White girl born and raised, but thanks for the compliment," Tiffany says, sitting between them as they dig into their meal. "In the before-times, I cooked and waited tables to pay my way through college."

"Cool," José says, scooping eggs, bacon, and potatoes onto toast. "What are you … what were you studying?"

"Psychology," she says. "I wanted … I want … to help people."

"Why, because no one helped you?" José asks half-jokingly, taking a bite from his pile of protein.

"Mom loved me plenty," Tiffany says, nibbling a strip of bacon. "Maybe too much, to make up for my father, who was never around. How about you? A tough guy from a rough part of town?"

"That's deep—and close," José says with a chuckle. He washes down his food with a slurp of coffee. "Mamá and Papá were hardly around, too busy working. My loving grandparents couldn't keep five grandkids out of trouble, especially me."

"Sounds right," she says with a grin. "How about you?" she glances at Myles. "What's your story, Ninja Stars?"

"You're never going to let that go, are you?" he says, chewing on his toast.

Tiffany sips coffee and waits for him to respond.

"I'm from a typical American family, I guess," Myles says. "My stepfather grew up poor, and he worked his way out of poverty by selling insurance. My mom was an elementary school teacher."

"And your father-father?"

Myles shrugs. "Not sure. Never in the picture, like yours. My mother hated to talk about him."

"Why did you two decide to work at camp?"

"Same reason as you," José says. "I wanna help others."

Tiffancy glances at Myles.

"To get out of the house," he says, "and figure out what I want to do with the rest of my life."

Tiffany's eyes brighten. "And?"

"Kill *Kiaskis*, of course," Myles says. "Seems like the only viable career option nowadays."

A round of laughter.

"I'm glad we had a chance to get to know each other better," Tiffany says, finishing her bacon, "before we die together."

The three Camp Friendly Forest counselors take a long look at each other.

No one laughs.

Throughout Friendly Forest, Myles, José, and Tiffany discover staff and children transfixed in that contagious state of paralyzed possession. Many, it seems, spent their final free moments engaged in activities typical of a summer day. These men and women, boys and girls, are positioned across basketball and tennis courts, baseball and soccer fields, in athletic wear and sneakers, eyes closed, arms and legs outstretched midstride, rackets and gloves in hand as they appear in rapt meditation, offering themselves up to the gods of death.

They find the expats—Scott, Richard, and Matt—huddled together behind the horse stables. Their backs pressed against each other, hands brandishing steak knives, raised high and ready to thwart an unseen foe. They look like statues of war heroes. At least they seemed to have left this world with a flicker of fight before they succumbed to despair.

Yet the *Kiaskis* are nowhere to be seen. What did these young men and women, boys and girls, observe or sense that propelled their psyches over the edge and give up on this existence? Did they spot the ravenous space dogs spying on them from the forest? Or was it some new, indescribable menace lurking in the shadows, pushing them into a trance, forcing them into another plane of awareness? If so, where are their minds now?

Myles, José, and Tiffany find more staff members and campers wading in the lake. Wearing boardshorts and bikinis, they stand waist-high in water, motionless, engaged in conversations no one can hear, that they will never complete. Smiles crack their lips, and they appear at peace, serene figures undisturbed by the lake's current. A baptism of acceptance, Myles realizes, inspired by doom, that defies the laws of gravity, entropy, or anything else that once made sense.

Finally, those who were less comfortable expressing their fear publicly are discovered alone, in closets and under desks, a last-ditch effort, perhaps, for their minds to find protection from an insidious incursion before they resigned themselves to the solace of surrender.

Everywhere the counselors wander, they witness human bodies immobilized in perpetuity, souls under siege. Eventually, Myles, José, and Tiffany enter *Whispering Dreams*. They find campers Myles has come to know well in the past week tucked in bunks, hidden beneath sheets that rise and fall in rhythm, a collective sigh of relief with each passing breath. The transformation of these individuals into undead corpses is jarring. Myles gently peeks under the sheets, half hoping his campers are playing a prank on him, and at any moment they will pop up from their beds with a hardy, "Surprise!"

No such luck.

They find Billy, in the bathroom, sitting on the toilet seat. He's wearing an Alien Logic T-shirt and pajama pants, tongue dangling from his lips, thumbs tapping on a tablet as he stares mesmerized at the images on the screen.

Myles opens the door wide, so José and Tiffany glean a better view. "How's it going, dude?"

"Okay, I guess."

Apparently, not even the imminent annihilation of the human race has affected Billy's superhuman apathy.

"My highest score in *Psycho Therapy*!" he shouts, and his enthusiasm — tied to a video game, startles them.

Billy hands Myles the tablet. At first, the counselor only sees black on the screen, which makes sense, because the wi-fi is dead and the camper's device should not be working. As Myles continues to peer into the display, however, lights and sounds appear that absorb his attention. Within the rectangular frame he spots … Billy … wearing the same Alien Logic T-shirt and pajama pants he has on in the bathroom. This Billy—inside the video game—also has large goggles wrapped around his head and a rocket pack slung around his back. His avatar zigzags back and forth among the Friendly Forest redwoods as *Kiaskis* leap from tree to tree, trying and failing to cling onto him. He laughs and zips past the alien monsters, incinerating them with laser beams that fire from his eyewear.

"This game is on a whole other level of crazy," José says.

In the background is a cabin with a mural Myles recognizes. Standing outside of *Whispering Dreams* are José, Tiffany, and himself dressed in the same Friendly Forest staff T-shirts they've been wearing since the invasion started. Their hands are raised as they cheer Billy to victory. Meanwhile, as Billy slaughters the cosmic canines, his high score flashes at the top of the screen.

Billy regards them with a grin. "Cool, right?"

Myles shakes his head in disbelief. *Are we just a bunch of characters in Billy's dumb video game?*

Explosions rock the cabin. The counselors step outside of *Whispering Dreams*. Myles half expects to see Billy flying around in his rocket pack, obliterating aliens with his laser goggles.

Instead, the glare of the setting sun blinds Myles for a beat, and he turns uneasily from side to side, hands raised, protecting his eyes, until he realizes what's happening. A camouflage Jeep pulls up to the camp's dusty parking lot. Four soldiers in fatigues step down, and one, a captain with a bandana wrapped around her head, directs a convoy of trucks behind them to stop. Out from three military transports hop dozens of Marines, armed and shouting as missiles explode along neighboring Shadow Mountain.

"Let's go, let's go, *let's go!*" she hollers, waving them toward fiery plumes rising in the distance. "The nest is five clicks that way! First one there gets to screw the Queen!"

An uproar of laughter from the Marines as they form up and fan out into the redwood forest. The captain turns, spots Myles and his friends, smirks, and follows her troops toward the action.

As José and Tiffany watch the firefight unfold, Myles realizes he is still holding Billy's tablet. He returns into the bathroom. Billy remains on the toilet seat with his proud grin, hands reaching toward Myles for his video game. His eyes are mostly closed, and a trail of vomit dribbles from his lips. Myles tries to revive Billy by shoving the device into his hands, but he can't. Billy's hands are stiff, as if already in a state of rigor mortis.

"Come on, dude!" Myles shouts.

No use. Billy's fingers are incapable of bending enough to receive his fix.

Myles steps outside and tosses the device into a bush.

"Billy's not joining us?" Tiffany asks as gunfire and screams ring in the distance.

"No," Myles says, shaking his head. "Billy is gone."

The commander guides Gus on a tour of the Institute.

The foyer is lined with portraits of former directors, and beyond the main hall, they find on walls macabre paintings, mostly of children dressed as clowns and circus freaks. They reach the cafeteria, where youthful laughter once echoed and mice droppings now litter tables. At the end of the dining hall, near the kitchen, is a dark stairwell, which Gus recalls leads to a belowground bunker, where many of Paranormal Plantation's VIPs were forced to reside, including himself. As Gus walks toward the steps, the commander places a hand on his shoulder. "That area is off limits, young man."

"Why?"

"After your ... evacuation ... no civilians have been permitted to be belowground."

Gus rolls his eyes. "Are there ghosts down there, or something?"

"Ghosts are the least of our worries."

As frightening a possibility as that may be, Gus is unwilling to let go of the stair rail, and his gaze remains fixed on the dark depths below. "Back when I cracked code in the basement down there, I used to hear yelling and screaming coming from the interrogation room. Wouldn't that be a good spot to place Alice and monitor her medical status?"

"Negative. You'll be lodged here on the ground floor, with me. Alice will be placed in the tower."

Thank you, Ray, for all I need to know. Following the commander back toward the cafeteria, Gus makes a mental note. *After so many years, the heart of this mad operation remains in the basement.*

As the battle for Shadow Mountain ensues, the Friendly Forest Few—as Myles refers to his conscious peers—rummage the military transports, searching for items they can use to defend themselves against their alien overlords. José opens a storage box filled with medicine and bandages. He stuffs them into a backpack. Tiffany pops the lock into a cabinet stacked with high-powered guns.

"I know this may feel like stealing, but it's not," she assures Myles as she straps a sniper rifle around her shoulder and grabs a carton of ammo. "As taxpayers, we're entitled to borrow this public property as long as we need it."

Myles flips over a seat and discovers a wrapped stick of gum.

"Can I keep this as long as I want it, too, or should I stick it back under the seat after I've chewed it?"

Laughter.

Tiffany hands Myles and José a tactical bowie knife. While admiring his blade's serrated edge, Myles sees a reflection of himself, including grays that have appeared over the past few days in his overgrown hair.

"Damn. I look old enough to get into a bar without being carded."

"No one's carding you," José says, revealing a bottle of tequila. "Should we make a toast?"

"Maybe when we have something to celebrate?" Tiffany says.

"Suit yourself," José says, taking a swig of the Central Valley's finest. "I'm going to enjoy this life while I can."

He offers the bottle to Myles, who passes. "Last person I shared a drink with—Geo, lost his mind, then his head."

"Suit yourself, buzz killer," José says with a smirk, capping the bottle and tossing it on a seat. "I hope you remember that drink you turned down with me when the *Kiaskis* are eating us alive."

"If that's my life's biggest regret, then it must be my time to die."

More laughs.

Tiffany holds her rifle high, eyeing through the scope, taking aim at an imaginary foe lurking outside the transport. "Wait … what?"

Myles glances her way and notices two sets of shoes scampering beneath the vehicle behind them. The three counselors hop out of the truck and pound along the cabin with their fists. "Who's there?"

At the rear, they find Tony and Post-Apocalyptic Girl. War paint streaks across their cheeks, and their over-sized fatigues have been torn and tied to fit their small frames.

Tony has a revolver raised. It trembles in his hands.

"José! Myles! Tiffany!" he shouts, lowering the gun. "Man, it's so good to see you!"

The two male counselors clasp Tony's shoulders, and Tiffany hugs Kylie. As the five of them relish their reunion, a ball of flame ignites the darkening sky, and thunderous roars from *Kiaskis* erupt in the distance.

"Is there any food left in the cafeteria?" Post-Apocalyptic Girl asks. "I'm hungry."

"More like hangry," Tony says. "Kylie and I have been bickering since we found each other hiding in an attic. We mustered enough courage to scout the camp, and we found the three of you huddled together, snoring away, and figured you were goners like everyone else around here. Have you seen Billy?"

"We did," José says.

"Is he still playing that crazy video game? *Psycho Therapy*?"

"Not anymore," Myles says. "It … he … finally shut down."

"Dang," Tony says. "I guess that's why that game's so popular … people get so addicted, they forget about living."

They forget about living. The idea lingers in Myles's brain. Isn't it strange that humans first contact with extraterrestrials happens to resemble their most dreaded concept of aliens from outer space?

From the forest stumbles forth the Marine Corps captain, bleeding from head, stomach, and legs. More *Kiaski* noise, a high-pitched war cry, resonates through a blackening terror-scape before them of war-ravaged forest. The howls from hell are deafening, and Myles and his friends cover their ears.

As the captain approaches, Myles follows her moving lips.

"We pissed off the Queen," she stammers, clambering into the Jeep. "That bitch and her damn space pups have taken over the Sierras. We're gonna blow a hole in these mountains. Only chance to prevent 'em … from swarming … Frisco … Vegas …"

Her eyes flutter, and her head falls forward on the steering wheel. José reaches into the Jeep and checks her pulse.

"Is she … asleep?" asks Kylie.

José nods.

There's the crack of branches, and five more wounded soldiers fumble from the forest. The slowest, carrying a high-caliber machine gun, stumbles into a patch of grass. As he tries to stand, reddish eyes gleam from the bushes, and there are growls around him. Three baby *Kiaskis*, each the size of a coyote, emerge from the shadows, extend their jaws and claws, and drag him back into the shrubs. The Friendly Forest Few listens to the man scream as he is devoured by the newborn monsters.

"Get out of my head!" Tony shouts, hopping into the back of the Jeep. With preternatural speed, he aims the gatling gun at the snarling shrubbery. The barrage of gun fire he unleashes sets off a series of shrieks along the edge of the forest. The half-eaten soldier emerges from the encroaching darkness long enough for Myles to see his shiny white teeth form a smile on his bloody lips. He pulls a grenade, tosses it behind him, and flops face down. Baby *Kiaskis*, buried in the bushes, wail from the explosion, and leaves are sliced and diced from Tony's stream of machine-gun rounds.

The Friendly Forest Few huddles behind the Jeep. When the ammo is finally spent, they rise. The immediate tree line has been razed to freestanding toothpicks. For a moment, all is quiet. A victory: the baby *Kiaskis* are dead. Just as Myles feels his body relax, the earth begins to tremble. Deafening howls and stomping paws. The violent collapse of entire redwoods. From the murky slopes of Shadow Mountain appear bopping heads and crimson glares, a horde of nightmarish extraterrestrials.

"Quick!" Tiffany screams. "Into the truck!"

In the blink of an eye, the Friendly Forest Few are buckled inside the nearest military transport. Myles feels like he's riding a roller coaster controlled by a carnival drunk. The pounding to the steel shell that contains them is relentless, and the advancing stampede knocks the vehicle from side to side, jarring him and his friends in their seats, rolling the truck several times before the ordeal comes to an end. Somehow, they manage to hold the contents of their stomach, but for several reasons, Myles doubts any of them will ever visit an amusement park again. He unbuckles his belt and crawls down from the side of the seat and out of the transport. Slowly, his friends join him. They stand and take stock of themselves and their surroundings. Each appears intact. As for the rest of their world …

Speechless.

The moon tears its way across a sky filled with bits of starry shrapnel that shine upon a flat and foreboding graveyard, a depressed and gutted no-man's-land that fans out forever and reflects the glimmering entrails of crushed infrastructure, razor-sharp teeth, and the blood and bones of people robbed of flesh, hope, humanity.

"It's like they took a bite out of everything—bark, buildings, bodies," Myles whispers. "No morsel left unturned."

"Except us," Tiffany says, turning to him.

"Except us," echoes José, turning to her.

"Except us," echoes Tony and Kylie, turning to José.

"Except us," Myles agrees.

As they stare at each other, face to face, the moonlight reflects their shared sadness. Wiping away tears, they stand, side by side, and determine what to do next. Turning their backs away from the carnage, the path becomes clear: Shadow Mountain, its streaks of jagged granite twinkling in the starry night, beckons with a mysterious majesty.

"I don't think anyone else is coming for the Queen," Myles says, holding Kylie's small hand.

"Agree," Tiffany, José, and Tony say at the same time.

"Except us," Kylie says, squeezing Myles's palm.

Myles glances down at her, returning the squeeze.

"Except us," he announces. "We leave at sunrise."

Chapter 18

Gus and Ray work to ensure that the Institute is online as quickly as possible. The commander, with an old, tattered blueprint in his hands, leads Gus on what feels like a grown-up treasure hunt through the haunted mansion. As they scour the property, they find ten generators housed in an off-site subterranean chamber. Only one of the generators, however, works. While Gus determines it powers the fountain of Jerome B. Goode, he realizes it lacks the energy to reboot the others.

"North America's top physicists will be arriving in the morning, and you're telling me we won't even be able to offer them a cup of coffee?" Ray asks, flashing a light on a patch of wires.

"Unless you intend to roast their coffee over a campfire," Gus says with a smirk. "Actually, that gives me an idea."

"I'm all ears."

"Back in the good old days—when I was a prisoner here—there was an old furnace in my cell. The furnace, apparently, had a dark history, to dispose of bodies of patients who didn't survive experiments conducted on them. Anyway, I might be able to relight that furnace and jerry-rig a device that captures enough heat that I can harness into a battery we can use to restart the other generators. To do it, you'll need to let me enter my old room, below the Institute. Nothing can be off-limits."

Ray regards Gus carefully.

"A brilliant idea," he admits. "Since I'm out of any, I guess we'll go with yours. Proceed."

Returning to the mansion, they shuffle past the cafeteria and creep down the stairwell into a pitch-black labyrinth. Moving forward, the commander insists Gus follow with a bandana tied around his eyes.

"You will get access to what you need, but I don't want you to know where we are going until we reach the furnace," he says. "This is a restricted area for a reason."

"Fine," Gus says, allowing Ray to blindfold him. "I spent my entire adulthood as a criminal hacker, but sure, I would hate to be accused of breaking any government regulations *now*."

Ray's flashlight, and Gus's hands, guide them along cement walls, corridors that echo their footsteps. The air is so musty that breathing is difficult. Mice squeak around their feet, and the blueprint takes them through a Cold War-era bunker, a legacy of the military industrial complex. They round a turn and are overwhelmed by light.

"I wasn't expecting it to be so … bright," Ray says, mesmerized. "The portal was sealed off after I evacuated you and your friends from the Institute."

"Portal?" Gus asks, assessing the bright patterns he gleans through the mask.

"There are several on Earth. Fortunately, all are under the purview of the North American Intergovernmental … my employer. This was the last portal we discovered, thanks to you."

"Me?"

"Your analysis of the Glitch led us to this location."

Gus realizes, among his buried memories, the reason he was brought to the Institute in 2026: to determine the source of the electromagnetic anomaly plaguing the United States. He was successful, too. The anomaly began in New York, spiraled across the continent, and ended at Paranormal Plantation.

"I see," Gus says, as Ray nudges him forward in his blindfold. "You didn't evacuate Alice and me and our friends from this awful place because you cared about our welfare. You freed us because you wanted to make sure we didn't interfere with … whatever is happening beyond that light."

Although he cannot distinguish details, the dazzling swirls of pinkish streaks ahead appear eerily familiar to Gus.

"Nothing is coming out of or going into that portal that the government hasn't authorized," the commander says, yet as he speaks, Gus is intrigued, his mind drawn closer and closer to the bewildering shimmer. "We're talking about a sealed doorway made with a double-plated saginium sheet that is ten-feet thick. That's more armor than what you'll find on a Liberator."

"Sounds … intimidating," Gus says, already imagining how he might bypass such an obstacle.

"Our safeguards are virtually impenetrable," Ray continues, guiding Gus along the corridor. "As you may have noticed, the military is so confident in its handiwork that it no longer occupies this mansion, and it would rather monitor this area from afar with satellites, and leave its secrets alone, than keep an in-person security detail present that would make it a target for Russian and Chinese spies. Frankly, Gus, not even you could crack the code on the panel down the hall that would allow the *Markahzi* to pass."

The *Markahzi*. The name makes the fugitive's legs wobble. They turn a corner, and the light from the portal fades as Ray removes the bandana from Gus's eyes and positions him inside his former cell. A hallucinogenic glow reflecting off the surrounding cinderblock walls is the only sign of any nearby source of enchantment, and it is enough to light the room.

Ray turns off his flashlight and flings his foot forward, kicking the remains of a busted door. Gus recalls that a girl named Melissa Vazquez turned the door into a heap with her telekinetic powers when she freed Gus from this prison a decade ago.

"Nothing's changed," Gus says, surveying the dingy bed, toilet, and out-of-date computer workstation, littered with old candy wrappers and empty cans of energy drinks.

"The military … had no need to change anything," the commander says. He bends down and clears the door debris with his hands, creating a clear path to the furnace. Gus joins him, and as they work, his mind teleports back to those tumultuous teenage months that he spent locked within this belowground installation, a captive tasked with cracking the code surrounding the Glitch.

Gus's servitude was supposed to be a fair exchange for a reduced prison sentence related to his involvement in the 2026 Bank Holiday led by the notorious Eco-Socialist renegade 'Che' Tay Wichmanowski. However, Gus was never formally charged for his involvement in that historic crime, nor was he officially detained by authorities. The Institute was a top-secret facility that ran as a top-down black site, defying the normal parameters of the law. There was no paper trail to track patient-victims.

That meant anything could go wrong at any time, with zero accountability, and indeed everything did. Locked-up in this basement-office-bedroom, tucked away in the Institute's sprawling underground complex, Gus lived off an endless supply of licorice and caffeine, allotted half-hour outings each day to breathe dry desert air and soak in enough sunlight to meet the government's minimal health requirements for Vitamin D. Outside is where he met other patients of Paranormal

Plantation and became acquainted with their exceptional abilities. The most famous, of course, was Alice Walker.

Gus's task was to determine any patterns related to the bizarre electromagnetic events disrupting the economy at the time. The Glitch was responsible for severe power outages in major cities across North America. Gus was so successful analyzing the Glitch through the outdated desktop computer before him now that he was able to confirm, through an algorithm he created based on a Fibonacci Sequence, the exact date and time that the paranormal power outages would conclude nationwide.

The final blowout occurred at the Institute itself, of course, where Gus and the rest of his gang of gifted misfits were detained. His simultaneous discovery of an impending incursion by an alien race—the *Markahzi*—prompted a revolt against the facility's authorities as the Glitch power outage ensued onsite. Thanks to the last-minute aid of then-Marine Corps Captain Ray Salvatore in his Liberator, Mama's Boy #1, Gus and his friends managed to escape from the perilous laboratory.

And the whole point of Gus's incarceration, and liberation, he realizes now, was to identify for the government the *Markahzi* portal so that it could be sealed.

He went his own way, and until Alice barged her way back into his life, he had enjoyed a quiet and unassuming career as a less-than-legal contractor through his company.

Little remained known to Gus about the alien race he fled at the Institute. However, he did know this much: Like the officials he mingled with over the years there, who defied the laws of the land, the *Markahzi* seemed to defy the laws of physics. According to the rumors he heard from his peers, the *Markahzi* exhibited incredible powers. Manipulating matter with their will, they were said to be master illusionists, who preyed on the minds of others. They were not defined by a form as much as a symbol, the third eye, displayed from time to time on the foreheads of their human hosts.

Since departing Paranormal Plantation, Gus has only seen the *Markahzi* in his nightmares, and he'd like to keep it that way.

The commander pushes the last of the debris out of the way, stands, and gestures toward the furnace. "Let's get those generators running, shall we?"

Work. Then, now, and forever—that's all anyone wants Gus to do. Stepping past Ray, the fugitive rubs the large pipes intersecting the wall. "Knock, knock," he says, opening the central heater where bodies once burned. "Anybody home?"

The only upside to the *Kiaski* stampede, and the destruction of Friendly Forest, is the ample kindling it provides. Tony and Kylie scour for clean clothes, which they find among the busted duffel bags and luggage of former campers scattered across the jagged reaches of demolished cabins. After doling out laundered T-shirts, socks, and underwear to Myles, José, and Tiffany, they dowse the rest of the clothes they find in gasoline, cut them into strips, and make torches. The rest of the clothing is stockpiled into a mound of fabric and used to keep their campfire crackling.

Tiffany, mind never straying far from food, locates in the vicinity of the crushed dining hall bottled water, canned goods, a Swiss Army knife, and eating utensils—the makings for a last supper. José successfully jumpstarts a military transport, the only one not turned upside down. Inside, he stockpiles guns, ammo, snacks, and drinks for tomorrow's trek to confront the Queen.

Myles surveys the rest of Friendly Forest for anything that might be of use for his peers' looming date with death. While the pickings are slim, he does discover Supernova Cid, buried between a busted desk and trampled clock. He brushes off the layer of crud caked on its glittery body and admires his childhood companion.

The gender non-specific figure was all the rage among children his age when he was growing up in the 2020s. With its amorphous silver space suit, short curly hair parted in the middle, and turquoise goggles and wristbands, Supernova Cid was the first 'non-binary' toy marketed as 'everyone's' superhero. Modeled off twentieth-century glam rock, the doll was especially popular, not only because of its inclusive ethos, but also due to its exotic characteristics, which no other children's toy has exhibited before or since.

"Guess what I found?" Myles hollers, holding the doll behind his back as he approaches the campfire.

"I'm afraid to ask," Tiffany responds as she warms cans of beans over the flames. "Ninja stars we can add to our arsenal of weapons?"

"Better," Myles says, thrusting the doll above his head for all to see, its glittery costume twinkling in the firelight. "I present to you an army of one. Ninja stars won't save us, Tiffany, but perhaps Supernova Cid will."

"Really?" José says with mild disappointment. He slams the hood of the military transport, brushes his hands. "Only hard-core nerds had that doll growing up."

"What is it?" Kylie asks, tossing a rolled-up bra into the fire, brightening the flames.

"Never heard of it," Tony says, abandoning fire to inspect the figure.

"Before your time," Myles explains, lowering the doll to his waist as the two kids scramble for a closer look.

"It's cute," Kylie says.

"It's gay, right?" José says.

"They're actually *non-binary*," Myles says.

"Does that make you uncomfortable?" Kylie asks, assessing José's response.

"Nah," José says, staring at the glimmering toy in Myles's hands. "When I was a boy, I was too busy doing bike tricks. I had no time to play with dolls—gay, straight, whatever."

Kylie stomps his foot.

"Ouch!" he squeals.

"Be nice!" she says.

"I *am* being nice," José says, assessing Kylie. "It's *true*."

Tiffany ventures away from her cans of beans to investigate.

"So soft," she says, rubbing Cid's slick suit. "It's cool you have one of these, Myles. Weren't they recalled?"

"They were," he says as the Friendly Forest Few take turns touching the vintage doll. "I just refused to let mine go. So, when Mom came rifling through my bedroom one day to send Cid back to the manufacturer, I told her I already threw mine away, but I kept it hidden in my closet until I felt it was safe to return the toy to my shelf. For Mom, it was out of sight, out of mind, until … recently … when she found Cid in my duffel bag for camp, and she realized we never parted ways."

"Feels nice," Tony concedes. "I don't understand. What's the problem?"

Myles squeezes Cid's stomach. Its goggles and wristbands glow, and the figure assumes a 'power stance'—hands on hips, feet shoulder width apart.

"I – AM SUPERNOVA CID!" the doll declares. "I EXPLODED INTO A SHOWER OF COLOR AND CREATED A MASSIVE BLACK HOLE IN THE CENTER OF THE GALAXY. WHY DO I MATTER? BECAUSE I *ATTRACT* MATTER!"

Supernova Cid locks eyes with the nearest member of the Friendly Forest Few, tears itself from Myles's fingers, and leaps onto José.

"I VANQUISH MY ENEMIES THROUGH THE POWER OF ATTTRACTION!" Supernova Cid announces, smothering the counselor's face with hugs and kisses. "LOVE IS LOVE—THE GREAT COSMIC EQUALIZER!"

"Ahhhhh!" José screams, yanking Cid off his head, slamming it onto the ground. "It's suffocating me!"

The glow of the goggles and wristbands fade, and the doll goes limp on the dirt.

Kylie and Tony converge, attempting to revive Cid, as José huffs. "What the hell was *that*?"

The two children pick up the doll off the ground, brush off the dust, and carefully return it to Myles.

"That, my friend," Myles says, "is an unsuspecting death trap."

Tony scratches his head. "They sold those to kids?"

"I'll explain during dinner."

"Great idea," Tiffany says. "Food's ready."

Chapter 19

The Friendly Forest Few slather beans on tortillas and roll them up into burritos while commiserating around the campfire.

"Tell us more about Supernova Cid!" Kylie insists.

"Yeah," Tony says. "Why does it try to hug everyone to death?"

Myles places the doll on a stump and squats next to it on a recovered lawn chair. "It was a marketing ploy that backfired. A doll that should have been accepted at face value turned into a corporate publicity scheme that created more division than unity, angering the very people they were trying to support. Shortly after the toy was released in 2026, when I was seven years old, a strange series of events took place ..."

"Stranger than mad dogs invading from outer space?" Kylie asks.

"Well, not that strange, but close," Myles clarifies. "Several unexplainable and unpredictable power outages started happening in cities across the country. At first, some people suspected they were cyberattacks caused by the Russians or Chinese, the usual suspects, but as time went on, and the outages continued, scientists admitted that they were no closer to understanding what caused them than they were when they first began.

They referred to these … energy irregularities … as the Glitch. Sometimes the outages lasted a few minutes, other times, for days."

Myles takes a bite from his burrito and pauses so the Friendly Forest Few can chew on the thought.

"Maybe it was caused by solar flares," Tony says.

"Maybe it was caused by global warming," Kylie says.

"The end of the world is upon us, and the kids are interested in atmospheric irregularities of yesteryear," José says.

"Shush!" Tiffany says to him. "It's a nice distraction."

"It's a distraction," José agrees, "but I wouldn't call it a *nice* one. Candy falling from the sky? Now, *that* would be a nice distraction."

A round of laughter.

"As you can imagine," Myles continues by the campfire, "the Glitch was a big deal. I can still remember my parents complaining when the blackouts occurred. During the energy disruptions, many day-to-day activities came to a halt. Lights went out, refrigerators shut off. No one could use the net. Even electric cars, suddenly drained of power, slowed to a stop in the streets with nowhere to charge. A lot of what happened was harmless, but not always. Airplanes, for example, that were flying in the radius of these energy disruptions fell from the sky and crashed. The economy was affected, and people became agitated, but for the most part, their health and well-being were spared. The biggest exception, it turns out, had to do with Supernova Cid …"

Myles takes a sip of water and gauges his audience. Tiffany is more interested in her food than his story, and José is more interested in Tiffany than his food, gazing at her across the fire, but Kylie and Tony are hooked. Myles, after all, remains the camp's designated Earth lore storyteller.

"The Glitch was often accompanied by unrecognizable sounds that not only caused electronic devices to malfunction, but once they were back online, they were sometimes altered and never performed the same."

Myles points at the unsuspecting doll propped up next to him. "When I received Cid as a Christmas gift, it was like reconnecting with a long-lost friend. When I snuggled with Cid, it purred like a cat. When I wanted to play with Cid, it talked back. The doll's greatest characteristic was the power of attraction: When I flung Cid against the refrigerator, it stuck to the panel and crawled right up to the top. The hands, you see, were made with powerful magnets."

"They attract matter!" Kylie says.

"Exactly," Myles says with a nod. "But when the Glitch started happening, something changed in the doll's programming. They lost a lot of functionality, as if they had been lobotomized. Cids became increasingly obsessed with the eyes, lips, and noses of anyone standing before them. Soon after the power outages began, there were reports of children being smothered by the 'deranged' toy."

"Creepy," Tony says.

"It was," Tiffany agrees, wiping her mouth with the back of her hand. "A girl in my class was hospitalized after being attacked by her Cid."

"For a doll the marketers promised would be 'everyone's' superhero, it wasn't long before Cids became the scourge of childhood. People who identified as non-binary, especially, felt misrepresented and betrayed."

"Like I said," José says, clasping his hands together with vindication. "I preferred sticking to bike tricks—"

"Why did you keep Supernova Cid?" Tony asks Myles. "Why did you lie and not give yours to your mom, when she came looking for it?"

"The same reason why I kept a shoebox filled with ninja stars under my bed," he says with a shrug. "Protection from intruders."

José rolls his eyes. Tiffany shakes her head. Kylie and Tony, confused, glance back and forth between the deactivated doll and its owner.

"Sorry, Mr. Harper," Tony says, breaking the silence, "but to keep a killer doll by your side all these years … that's kind of cringy."

"Yeah," Kylie says. "Why did you bring Cid to camp? That's even *more* cringy."

"I thought it would be fun to show off, then toss in a campfire."

"Well, there's a campfire," José says, pointing. "Maybe it's time to let go."

Myles removes Cid from the stump. He imagines watching his childhood companion burn.

"Not today," he says, holding the doll in his hands. "Supernova Cid's come this far without doing me wrong. I'll save mine for the *Kiaskis*."

"There ya go," José says with a fist pump. "Annoy 'em to death!"

Chapter 20

Toiling through the night, Gus manages to reboot the Institute's power by dawn. He and the commander scramble up the stairwell, above the first and second floor, to the tower. They arrive in time to watch the shutters of the panoramic windows automatically respond to the sunrise and slide open.

As the morning light shines through the circular tower, Gus sees Alice, strapped to a gurney, surrounded by electronics springing to life. Her medical team, a doctor and two nurses, assess the monitor's readings that activate by her side.

"All vital signs remain stable," the doctor says.

The baldheaded woman with black bushy brows, who resembles an Egyptian pharaoh in a lab coat, prepares a syringe.

"What are you doing?" the commander asks.

"Something we should have done long ago," she says. Inside the syringe, Gus spots a tiny silver chip. "A tracer, so we'll never lose Alice again."

"Alice wouldn't approve," the commander says.

"Of course, she approves," the doctor corrects him. "*Nothing* happens to Alice that she isn't already aware of, sir. We are playing catch-up with our actions to the reality *she* has already prepared for us."

"That's a weird justification for unsolicited government meddling," Gus says, unable to resist the urge to interrupt them.

"Perhaps, but it's true," the commander says after considering the possibilities. "Proceed, doctor."

The pharaoh-looking medical practitioner injects the chip into Alice's neck. For an instant, Alice appears to flinch. However, the team continues with their work, and even the commander and the machines hooked up to the psychic fail to register the change in her disposition.

Did I just see Alice wince? Gus thinks to himself. *Is she even asleep? And if she isn't asleep, why would she spend days pretending to be?*

"There it is," the commander says, stepping toward the expanded window. Gus glances up from Alice and sees what the military man sees: a great wall of extraterrestrial light rising from the desert sand, draped like a giant shower curtain over the southern slopes of the Sierras. He also realizes where he has seen that same pattern of light. Downstairs. The portal. "Just in time," the commander says. "Our team is here."

In the distance, a Chinook helicopter accompanied by a Liberator appear as growing dots along the kaleidoscopic veil. Gus steps toward a computer console and proceeds to type furiously.

"What are you doing?"

"Pulling up data I collected after my van crashed," the hacker says.

Superimposed over the left side of the tower window is a close-up of the Spectacle, video footage taken from Gus's drone. Superimposed on the right side of the tower window is a graph of the drone's infrared readings. Their real-time view of the anomaly remains visible in the window between.

"The shimmering light we see contains every wavelength of radiation found in our cosmic signature," Gus says, pointing at the bands of color on the graph. "In other words, the Spectacle seems to be reflecting *all* light—not just visible light—sent its way."

"What are you trying to say?" the commander asks. "Keep in mind, Gus, I've only passed college-level physics."

"Because the Spectacle only reflects light from our dimension, and it does not seem to *generate* any light on its own ... whatever is happening inside the veil ... well, it's not part of our reality."

"Are you saying the Spectacle is a ... fabrication?"

"To use a term appropriate for the desert—yes, sir—I believe what we're seeing is a mirage."

The commander's façade cracks. "The Pentagon calls it the Zone of Proximate Experience."

"ZoPE ... at least that acronym has a nice ring to it," Gus says, "unlike others used in your government lexicon." He points at the anomaly of light. "Be honest, Ray, this next-level tech the military has been pumping out for the past few decades, it comes from *them*, doesn't it? Your Liberator, for example, it really *is* out of this world."

"Early this century, a military engineer, Stephen Humphrey, accidentally fell into a portal while he was hiking," the commander says. "That's when we first learned of *their* existence. He eventually emerged from the portal, and when he did, he was different. He knew how to make things, powerful things. The Pentagon has never been the same."

He regards Gus carefully. "That's top-secret tech information that even a hacker as good as you probably never cracked. So, the question is, how did you know?"

"I see them in my dreams."

The commander takes a step back. "Say again?"

"The *Markahzi*," Gus says, "I've been dreaming about them and their weapons of war since my release from the Institute. The nightmares haunt me no matter how hard I try to forget about my experiences … here."

"You see them in your dreams?" the commander clarifies.

"All the time," Gus says with a twinge of sadness.

The commander points to the exit as if admonishing a misbehaving dog.

"Thank you for your service, Gus, but you must leave this tower immediately," he says, and into his lapel, "Mama's Boy #1 to base. We have a suspected high-level *Markahzi* outbreak underway. We're going on lockdown."

An immediate response broadcasts across Paranormal Plantation: "COPY COMMANDER RAY SALVATORE. INITIATING QUARANTINE PROTOCAL M-A-5-K-9."

Outside the window, Gus sees the approaching black Liberator touch down in a nearby field, causing the tower to tremble. Meanwhile, the helicopter, containing the scientists, pulls away and vacates the area.

The commander signals the nurses, who step to the side of Alice and pull up their sleeves. They reveal themselves to be two buff soldiers with brawny, tattooed arms.

"These men will keep an eye on you for the remainder of your stay."

"If it's all the same to you, Ray, I'd rather hitchhike home than stick around here …"

"Sorry, Gus," the commander says with a pitiful stare. "If you've been infected by the *Markahzi*, you cannot share the same space as Alice, nor can you leave this facility. I'm afraid you must remain here for a while longer."

"Infected?" Gus asks, patting himself with paranoia.

"You'll be free soon."

The soldiers grab Gus, and they lead him away.

"That's what you *say!*" Gus shouts, struggling to escape as he is forced down the stairwell, "but it's what you *do* to me, Ray, that matters!"

José drives.

Tiffany rides shotgun. She helps to navigate the transport's over-sized tires through a path of jagged junk and razed trees. In the back, Myles, Tony, and Kylie figure out how to load weapons without access to a BoobTube tutorial. Besides a Beretta and twelve-gauge shotgun, Myles settles on a tomahawk, a camp favorite.

The rumbling of the engine is loud, too loud to talk civilly, so they shout, unwilling to spend their final hours in silence.

Tony gets to the point. "What's the plan?"

"You're asking, *now?*" José hollers from the driver seat, chewing bubble gum. "Simple: kill until you can't kill any more."

"You make it sound like we're auditioning for an action movie," Tiffany says, hands propped up on the dashboard, painting her fingernails.

"What is this life, if not a movie?" wonders José, with a hint of frustration. "A suicide-mission?"

But it's not a conversation anyone wants to have. José switches into low gear as the transport rumbles up a rocky hill. "Sorry, folks," he says, lightening up. "I guess I left my helpful guide, *How to Beat the Kiaskis with a Positive Attitude*, back in L.A."

Myles, Tony, and Kylie watch in the rearview mirror as José blows a bubble with his chewing gum that pops on his cheeks.

"Maybe you're right," Tiffany says, dropping her hands from the dashboard. "Maybe we should treat this … mission … as if we're starring in a movie? Doesn't that mean the villain … the … Queen … should have a weakness?"

"I saw a *Kiaski* light up nicely when its body caught fire," Myles says, remembering the monster that consumed Geo. "Maybe their pelts don't mesh well with our atmosphere?"

"You mean they're flammable, or something?" José says. "Maybe. In that case, hopefully some grenades will put her down."

"Hopefully," Myles says, thinking out loud, "but something about this … war … has been troubling me since it started …"

Tiffany glances at him in the rearview mirror. "Yeah, we're losing."

A round of laughter.

"Nah, something else," Myles says. "Something deeper."

"A whole species faces genocide," José says, punching the gas as the transport flops over a tree trunk. "I'm not sure anything gets deeper than that."

Myles's eyes stray from the vehicle's path. He sees a family of bears, their bodies eviscerated by the *Kiaskis*, attracting a swarm of flies. It is probably the remains of the same bears he encountered under the stars, now roadkill from an alien stampede. Maybe this is just nature's way, one alpha species being supplanted by another one, but so much death seems unreal, and unnecessary, just to make a point. A thought occurs to him. "Do any of you remember *how* this war started?"

"News reports," Tiffany says, finishing her nails.

"No, it started with that strange light in the forest," Tony says. "Remember?"

"True," José says, steering the transport over boulders. "But this war started before that, really, when you think about it. It started with a popular video game. It started with *fear*."

"Fear of what?" Kylie asks.

"Fear of the unknown," Myles says. "Fear of what extraterrestrial life might be like. Fear of what might happen to us when we make contact."

"And for good reason," José says. "Contact has been an otherworldly nightmare. Too strange to seem possible."

Too strange to seem possible, Myles repeats to himself. He recalls Alice's warning: *Mind your escape. Maybe our minds ARE our escape?*

Tiffany turns back to show off her fingernails: ten black and white skull-and-bones. "Aren't they pretty?"

"Pretty ugly," Myles says.

A round of laughter.

"Cool!" Kylie says, flashing Tiffany her own unadorned digits. "Will you do mine, too, please?"

Tiffany smiles at the child in a camouflage T-shirt with peace-sign pins adorning her shoulders. "Sorry, girl, but I prefer you just as you are."

Kylie withdraws her fingers. A tear rolls down her eye. "That's something my mom would say."

Tiffany faces forward. Awkward. As much as they try to avoid silence, silence comes for them. Myles wants to think more about the *Kiaskis*, their origins, and their purpose, but he and the rest of the Friendly Forest Few are distracted. Kylie's sniffles drown their thoughts, but no one can stomach looking her in the eye, except José.

"Your mom would be proud of you," he says, gazing at Kylie in the rearview mirror. "That camo you're wearing can't hide what you are inside."

"And what's that?" Kylie says, looking up at him.

"A girl ... with a big heart."

"Is that all?" she responds, wiping away her tears.

José stops chewing his gum. "And a girl with ... impeccable fashion taste?"

Kylie raises her eyebrows, folds her arms, waits.

"And ... incredible sense of humor?"

"And?"

"Amazing conversational skills?"

She smiles. "Okay, that's better."

A round of laughter.

"Good, because I was running out of compliments," José says with a grin.

More laughter.

Tiffany squeezes José's hand and whispers 'thank you' as the transport putters to a halt. Myles waits half-expecting them to kiss. Instead, the foulest of odors, a savage cloud of flatulence, permeates the air. José tries to play it cool with a shrug and restart the vehicle, but it's no use. The silent-but-deadly fart is grounds for immediate evacuation. "I guess this is the end of the line," he says flatly.

"Great, get us outta here!" Tony squeals, the first to hop out of the transport.

"Gross!" Kylie declares, waving a hand in front of her nose.

The rest of them disembark. Far from camp, above the tree line, they are surrounded by boulders leading up to steep granite walls. The sun beats bright, its scorching light unfiltered by clouds and the lack of shade. The stench persists.

"Damn, who did that?" José demands. "Something up here stinks."

"I figured it was you," Tiffany says.

"Not my brand," José says, and with no one amused, he changes the subject. "We're approaching the top of Shadow Mountain," he says, glancing up the slope like a reluctant tour guide. "From here, we hike."

Not everyone is ready to move on.

"There must have been so many *Kiaskis*, to knock down so many ancient, mighty trees," Tony says, nostalgically gazing down the path of expanding flattened timber. "Strange. I don't see any signs of *Kiaskis* up here. Do you?"

There's a minor explosion—a nasty ripper—that reverberates from up the mountain and out of sight. The Friendly Forest Few grabs their gear and scrambles up the slope.

They find a sulfuric-smelling mass of red organic matter, like a giant smashed tomato, piled on top of a boulder, which overlooks a precipice.

"Smells like one seriously nasty turd," Myles says, holding his nose as the oval mass begins to unfold like a flower. From within, a baby *Kiaski* emerges. The cluster of reddish eyes blink as they adjust to their first light, and the head lifts, sniffing the air, sensing the humans. The eyes fix on Kylie, the nearest potential meal as its long tongue slithers out from the tiny tot's over-sized lips toward the child's legs …

"*Ahhhhh, it's sooooo cuuuuute!*" Kylie says with a beaming smile, her high-pitched Valley Girl dialect a badge of honor that she no longer tries to hide. As Myles steps forward to prevent her from petting the creature, she raises her Uzi. Her smile fades. "You took my mommy, my daddy, my brother, my dog, my cat, my friends, and everything I love in this world, but you're not taking me, little monster!"

She opens fire. The tiny *Kiaski* squeals, pushed back from the barrage of bullets, clinging for dear life on the edge of the precipice.

"Die, you little furball!" she screams, continuing to unload until, finally, the baby alien's pelt proves to be no match for the mini machine gun. As the space pup slips off the side of the ridge, its innards explode. The Friendly Forest Few stares from the ledge at the splattered black and white bits of floating extraterrestrial guts.

"You killed one!" Tony shouts.

"I can't believe it!" Tiffany hollers.

They huddle together, overjoyed with excitement.

"All right," José says with a sober calm. "At least now we know they can die."

There's a growl. They glance up. Gazing down at them from the ledge above is another baby *Kiaski*, barely able to see, licking the air, tongue winding down like a snake searching for them. Next to it, is another.

And another

And another.

And another.

"Let's rock!" José hells, tossing a grenade up the slope.

They take cover against a wall of granite.

BOOM!

Rocks tumble and newborn monsters fall from above, smashing onto boulders, plunging to their deaths. The Friendly Forest Few fires at will as young *Kiaskis* kamikaze them from all sides. The space pups blink and bark as they drop from the sky, stumble around corners, and clamber up rocks. Myles and his friends blast them into chunks of blotchy flesh, baby carnivores from another world that fail to ground themselves in this one as they are forced off the slope and plummet to oblivion.

But there are too many, and the only option is retreat.

José points, leading their escape. "Into that cave!"

Chapter 21

Commander Ray Salvatore didn't have the courage to be honest with Gus. He sits at the center workstation of the tower, Alice's unconscious body lying in the gurney behind him, the view of the anomaly rising before him, regretting the order he must give the two soldiers. As he waits for critical reports to upload onto the computer, he feels like a commander, not of an elite military unit, but one navigating a starship through a spectacular nebula. "So beautiful," he mutters, gazing out at the celestial wall in the distance. "I wish Sara could see it."

"I'm sure she and a few billion others are gazing at it right now through their social media feeds and transforming the images into cat memes," the doctor says, resting her hand on the commander's shoulder. "I'm sorry, Ray, but you have to kill that young man."

Ray rubs his temples, but it does little to relieve the pressure building in his head. "I was just bragging to Gus how I'm trying to save more lives than I take."

"We can't risk the outbreak," the doctor says, massaging his neck. "To prevent the spread, we must eliminate all hosts."

The preview of the NAITFSD's latest report populates on the screen: *Official Threat Readiness Guide for Worlds War One.*

"And what happens if thirty million *Markahzi* demons, disguised as Southern Californians, march out of that Spectacle, ready to take on the human race?"

"There are protocols in place."

"Easy for you to say, Jane," Ray snaps, flicking her hand off his neck as he reads the italicized phrase, *eradication by any means necessary.* "You're not the one who would have to pull the trigger on so many lost souls."

To the untrained ear, the 'sigh' from the doctor that follows would probably indicate that she is unimpressed with the commander's response to his moral dilemma. However, to Ray's trained ear, that 'sigh' is in fact a gasp caused when an individual skilled in martial arts chokes a victim into submission.

Immediately, Ray rips the computer screen off the counter, removing the classified document from sight, and leaps forward, rolling off the side opposite the workstation. He turns to find Alice standing in her patient gown, watching him, and the doctor slumped behind her, lying unconscious in the gurney.

The psychic smiles. "It's time to normalize extraterrestrial life."

Ray raises his fists. "I can't let you do that, Alice. If we let them breed *through* us, they will breed us *out.*"

"The invasion cannot be stopped," Alice says. "It can only be mitigated. Trust me."

"Just like you asked me to 'Trust Gus'—a *Markahzi* host?"

"I didn't write that in my notebook. Gus did."

"Even worse, because you *knew* he would write it," Ray says, "just like you knew I would fall for it … just like you feigned unconsciousness … without anyone's knowledge … so that you and Gus would be brought here, and do what?"

It occurs to him.

"Enter the portal," he says, eyes flickering as he rattles off the scenario in his mind. "Of course. But why *this way*, Alice? You could have driven right into the Spectacle yourself, if you were so curious, without risking anyone else's life."

The young woman, even while wearing a patient's smock, exudes a supernatural confidence. "It's not just about *how* I enter," she says. "It's about *when* and *with whom* I enter. To save *us*, I need *them*."

"Who?" Ray asks.

"The Initiates," Alice says. "Our planet's greatest hope. Lower your fists, commander. You can't hurt me. I've seen this moment play out a million times. You didn't even know it was coming."

"I would never try to hurt you, Alice," Ray says, bracing for a fight, "just defend myself against you."

"Liar," she says, kicking the workstation into his shins. The pain from the impact to the commander's legs causes him to buckle, and he leans forward just close enough for Alice to grab his lapel. She rolls over the workstation and returns to a standing position with his communicator in her hand. She drops the device on the floor and smashes it with her bare heel.

The commander lunges toward her. She swerves around him, pulls the patient gown off her body, and wraps it around his head. He tears the gown off himself as he sprints to the door.

"You're too fast," he says, panting, blocking the exit.

"I just see too much," she says, walking toward him in a tank top and underwear. "I see what you're going to do in a second, a month, a year."

He swings, misses.

"A year, huh?" he asks, swinging and missing again. "So, you're saying I have a future?"

"We all do," Alice says, outmaneuvering his punches and kicks. "But we must never stop *working* toward it. Tomorrow is as fragile as today."

"You sound like a fortune teller who leases one of those shabby retail spaces at an outlet mall."

"In that case, let me offer you some free advice, Ray, so we can end this reunion quickly, because it's been three days, and I really need to pee."

"Go on," Ray says, extending a right hook, a left upper cut.

"Take your daughter, Sara, to Europe," Alice says, dodging his blows. "Show her the museums, while you can. Let her bask in the art and architecture. Enjoy your time together. You won't always be the only man in her life."

"What's that supposed to mean?" Ray asks, kicking air. "Is Sara going to have a boyfriend soon?"

"Maybe she already does, and she just isn't ready to tell you," Alice says with a grin. "Two more points for you, Daddy-O, if you pay for *them* to go *together*."

"Never!" Ray shouts. He flails his arms and legs in a desperate assault, panting, sweating, and avoiding Alice despite his intense efforts. Fatigued, he changes his mind. "Okay, maybe if he proves *worthy* enough to *marry* Sara, I *may* pay for their honeymoon."

"Now you're talking," Alice says as Ray again lunges toward her. She grabs his right wrist and turns him around, activating a pressure point, and strikes down on his elbow with her knuckles, activating another. She punches his exposed ribs, activating a third pressure point, and causing his legs to collapse, bringing him to his knees. She whacks his neck, and he falls unconscious next to the doctor.

"Sleep tight," she says. "When you wake, commander, you'll have saved more lives than you ever imagined."

The Friendly Forest Few burrows inside the cave, creating a line of fire against the advancing space pups.

"Keep 'em dropping!" José commands. The alien newborns scramble over each other half-blind, searching for human flesh with their slobbery snouts and slithery tongues, crying out as they are mowed down by a hail of gunfire. As the pile of furry bodies grows higher and higher, it cuts off more and more sunlight leading into the cave. "Explosives, hurry!"

Kylie and Tony unzip a duffel bag stuffed with claymore mines and hand grenades. José covers Myles with rounds from an M-16 as the counselor from West Hollywood sticks his tomahawk in his belt and plants a charge on top of the *Kiaski* carcasses. Their unopened eyes and lippy grins, Myles realizes, makes them seem like they're dreaming when they're dead. Sliding down from the stack of blotchy, bloody pups, Tiffany tosses a grenade and yells, "Duck!"

A one-two punch of explosions rips through the entrance of the cave, causing rocks to crumble, dust to scatter. Myles trips and plunges face-first into a ditch, head smacking into a slab of granite. As his brain rattles, he mistakes the darkness that surrounds him as a sign he has died. As the debris settles, however, and his brain does the same, he hears Kylie and Tony coughing nearby. Two headlamps turn on, and he vaguely identifies the figures of José and Tiffany, each stumbling toward each other.

Myles realizes that while he and his friends may have thwarted off the *Kiaski* onslaught, they have also sealed their fate, entombing themselves inside Shadow Mountain.

"Myles?"

"Over here."

They fumble over the rugged interior his way. Two bright beams shine on his contorted frame.

For a moment, silence.

"That bad?" he asks.

Kylie and Tony shake their heads, not in disgust, but dismay, and Myles realizes his condition must be even worse than he assumed. The side of his face is wet, so he dabbles it with his hand and licks the salty blood dripping from a gash in his head. His friends stare at him as if they have just discovered a vampire unearthed from a grave.

"Not good," Tiffany says.

José hops down into the ditch and extends a hand. "You probably won't be winning any beauty contests soon, but you already knew that. Never really a contender."

Myles laughs and uses José's extended hand to hoist himself into a standing position, but he can't manage to stay upright. Best he can do is prop himself on his right leg and lean against the slab of granite. A throbbing sensation creeps up his left leg, a ghost limb he can't shake. "Something's wrong."

"There's the understatement of the year," Tiffany says, flashing her light around Myles's body.

"There!" Tony points.

A puss-filled tongue has coiled itself around Myles's ankle. From several buds, each the size of a baseball, countless tiny barbs poke out and penetrate his skin—a prickly cactus from the wrong side of the cosmos.

"Can you move?" Tiffany asks.

Myles tries pulling his left leg away from the fleshy snare, but the tongue responds instinctively by tightening its grip, and the barbed intrusions stab deeper into his dermis. Around the wound, a black, pulsating liquid begins to fill his veins, a dark, milky puss that slowly traces its way up his shin toward his thigh.

"Come on, do something!" Kylie shrieks, surveying the spread of the infectious substance.

José and Tiffany shine their headlamps on Myles's left ankle, following the long winding tongue under their legs, along the cave floor, to a baby

Kiaski. A fallen boulder separated its torso from its head, and the tongue rolls out from the mouth like a vile celebrity carpet in desperate need of a guest.

"It must have lassoed your leg just as it was decapitated," José says, stepping back from the disembodied cranium. "Smells like a rotten watermelon."

"Don't worry, I'll set you free," Tiffany says, withdrawing a hand-ax from her belt and slicing the fatty tube of flesh.

The severed tongue slackens, followed by a high-pitched scream: "ICK-NYEEEEET-CHEEEEE-KA-LEEEEEE!"

The decapitated pup's lids open, revealing clusters of reddish eyes, and the mouth expands, causing the boulder to roll off the dismembered head, revealing its first row of razor teeth. Kylie grabs a grenade from the duffel bag and pitches it into the drooling orifice. The newborn monster wails with primal defeat up to the instant it explodes, showering the Friendly Forest Few with disgusting debris.

With the pup's destruction, and the separation of its tongue from Myles's leg, they notice with their shining lights that the inky fluid filling Myles's skin starts to fade.

"Better," Myles says, limping forward, leaning on Tony with one hand, withdrawing the tomahawk from his belt with the other. "Thanks, team. Time to level up."

Guided by the headlamps, the Friendly Forest Few courses through the rocky tunnel, feeling their way forward with their hands and feet, avoiding any occasional pitfalls that might further jeopardize their lifespan. The path is uncertain and increasingly wet, with black-and-white goo dripping from the walls, slime sticking to their fingers and shoes.

"I don't like this," Kylie says with a huff. Instead of grumbling further, she checks the status of her Uzi. Loaded. "At least I have a never-ending supply of ammo."

"I guess that's a perk," José says, "when your alien overlords turn your life into a video game."

Tiptoeing forward, they follow Kylie's lead: daggers, explosives, hatchets, and guns ready. The path along the cave becomes warm, a crimson glow beckoning them from around a bend.

"Is that an exit ahead?" Tony asks, his tone conveying both an honest question and desperate comment.

"That," Tiffany says, wiping her brow, "or by now we've reached the center of the Earth."

"I bet you by the time we dig ourselves out of this cave," José says, "we'll be in China."

"Maybe the *Kiaskis* won't bother us there," Tony says. "I always wanted to try dim sum."

"In that case, we just need to take a field trip to Lee's Restaurant in downtown L.A.," Myles says.

"Maybe after a shower," Tiffany says.

"And after they rebuild L.A.," José says.

They reach a sprawling cavern adorned with stalactites and discover the source of the crimson glow: a vast pool of radiant light.

"Is that lava?" Tiffany wonders. Her drenched Camp Friendly Forest T-shirt, previously a dirty-green, now shines with a spectacular fluorescence. She stops and admires everyone else's garb. "All of you … look … so … stellar."

"At least it's now bright enough to see where we're going," José says, shutting off his headlamp. "I was getting tired of squinting."

He opens a bottle of water, takes a swig, and passes it around. They take turns rehydrating, contemplating their opportunities to escape this natural furnace and enjoying the glow of their clothes. Kylie and Tony look the most distinguished. Their camouflage T-shirts shine like a neon rainbow with mixed layers that resemble a jade forest, golden sunlight, and tropical ocean. Even Kylie's peace-sign pins glitter, playing deceptive tricks on the eyes, each spinning in unison like a spoke wheel of love.

"What *is* this place?" Tony wonders.

THE END, a clear, authoritative voice echoes through their minds.

They step closer together. A gigantic *Kiaski*, shaped like a dragon, emerges from the pool. Its face is a shadowy mass topped with jutting horns and a forehead filled with crimson eyes that blend into a long, gigantic snout and mouth, with feathery fur that forms a beard around a pointy, fiery chin.

Kylie gasps, staring frightfully at the creature. "Is that the Devil?"

Chapter 22

One way or another, Gus should have known big government would orchestrate his return to this dingy dungeon. At least he managed to power the Institute, making visible with its lights just how depressing his purgatory is. The Cold-War era cinderblock walls, cement floors, and ceilings have stood the test of time with only a few cracks revealing its faulty foundation.

Sitting on this ancient, rickety bed and twiddling his thumbs, for Gus there seems to be two distinct possibilities how the next few minutes of his life will unfold. The first and most likely scenario: *Commander Ray Salvatore, who suspects because of my dreams that I am now a Markahzi host, will order his guards to enter this cell and send me on a one-way trip to eternity.* The second, less likely scenario: *Alice Walker, the legendary 'psychic'—who has only proven to me over the course of our 'friendship' that she has an exceptional ability to trigger my anxiety—will walk through that busted door and force me to persevere in her adventure.*

Gus shakes his head. Enough with binary thinking. He doesn't believe in such strict parameters around reality. Hell, he's the world's greatest code breaker. He reminds himself that bending the rules is his happy place.

Hunger must be clouding his judgment. Glancing at his old workstation, he sees countless mice droppings along with ravaged bags of potato chips and discarded licorice wrappers, but no signs of food that is currently edible.

"Hey, got any snacks?" he hollers to the guards outside the cell. The peculiar light from the Spectacle refracts mystically over the cracks on the walls. "I thought this resort package I purchased included room service?"

One of the guards, face marked with acne, pokes his head inside and tosses Gus a granola bar.

"Thanks," Gus says.

The last supper.

The hacker wonders if his death is part of Alice's plan, like others who have come and gone from her orbit, a pawn to be sacrificed on her path to victory … *whatever that is.* Saving the world from an alien invasion? Please. *Try saving us, Alice, from ourselves.* If extraterrestrials don't destroy humanity, humanity is well on its way to destroying itself and its earthly habitat. *Even the great revolutionary of last decade—my comrade, Che Tay—as well as our greatest nemesis, James Elroy, became victims of your time-transcending ambitions, Lady Prophet. Why should I be less fortunate than they were?*

A scuffle ensues outside the cell.

"She's conscious!" a guard shouts.

"Commander's signal has been compromised!" shouts the other guard. "Engage, but do not harm her!"

Sneaking to the doorway, Gus peeks down the illuminated hall. Alice stands at the bottom of the stairwell, her patient's smock replaced with her overworn red hoodie and jeans. She engages in hand-to-hand combat with the two soldiers. As fast as the military men move – kicking, swinging, and attempting to pin her down—she easily evades them.

It's like she sees them coming from a mile away. Psychic? Impossible, but perhaps a master in kung fu with the reflexes of a hummingbird.

The two guards fall flat on each other with an anti-climactic thud. Gus steps into the hallway.

"You're awake."

"You're observant," she says, catching her breath.

"You've been awake *this whole time*! You flinched when the medic injected you with the tracking chip, didn't you?"

"I see nothing gets past you," she says, looking past him at the portal. "No wonder they say you're one of the smartest people in the world."

"Not really. You tricked me. You left me worried sick as I traipsed around the Central Valley with you hitching a ride in the back of my van like your personal, unpaid, creepy chauffeur."

"Thank you," she says. "For *everything*." She waits for a beat. "May we proceed?"

"No!" Gus stammers. "We may not proceed! My van is trashed, stuck in a ditch. You owe me for mileage, wear-and-tear, loss of use … and an explanation of what the hell you want, for now and eternity!"

Alice walks past the hacker and into a spectrum of color, a prism that radiates around the silhouetted edges of a vault. He follows her, stepping before the sealed portal, admiring the waxy material that is said to be impenetrable. Liberator stuff. Otherworldly stuff. Even the control panel doesn't make sense: a blank display with no prompts or keypad that would cause a migraine for many hackers, but not Gus. Not this time.

"The commander says it's impossible to crack."

"In that case," Alice says, a glaze over her eyes, her mind already elsewhere, "you can wait for him to wake and be greeted with whatever fate he has in store for you, a *Markahzi* host—orrrrr …"

"Orrrrr, what?"

"Open the portal, Gus. Honor the memory of your deceased grandfather, who you adored, and save your race."

A punch to the gut about his grandfather. "If you know so much … why not just open it yourself?"

"Quit playing games," she says. "You know why."

The truth feels like an electric shock tingling up his spine. He *does* know why.

"Because … I never show you how," he says.

"In all of the timelines of the multiverse," Alice says, "you may not be able to see the future, Gus, but you do have an exceptional ability to safeguard your self-interest. Now it's time to be vulnerable, open yourself up. To me."

The portal, like the Spectacle itself, is an illusion. It's not about what's there. It's about what we think *is there.*

Gus reaches over to Alice with his left hand and covers her eyes. He shuts his own. Mesmerizing rays dance on his retinas. Soon, the question of whether his eyes are closed or open no longer makes a difference. The vault splits in half, beckoning him like the parted gates of heaven.

"Go," he says, his hand falling to his side, squeezing hers. "Perform your miracles, Alice. Save us."

"I didn't need you to open the portal for *me*," she says, clenching his hand, guiding him forward. "I needed you to open it for *you*."

The Queen's tail extends out from the pool, covered with golden scales and black pods. The black pods blink haphazardly, little eyeing blobs creating the odd illusion of a starry night twinkling in a far-flung universe. They excrete a reddish poop, the mother *Kiaski's* spawning material, likely, which her flapping appendage thrashes around and smears like paint against the canvas of the cave.

"If she's the Devil, I guess those are … deviled eggs?" Kylie says with a snort, pointing at the bloody clumps.

There is a round of laughter as the Friendly Forest Few sluggishly raises their guns, ready for a final dog fight.

The Queen's snout protrudes from her feathery face, a fat pole of sniffing slobber under which a mouth filled with silvery, jagged teeth forms a crooked grin. *THERE IS NO STOPPING YOUR ENDING, JUST AS THERE IS NO CONTINUING YOUR BEGINNING*, her voice echoes in their heads while her lips remain fixed in that awful smile. *YOUR SPECIES CAVES TO THE TERROR IT HAS CREATED. THE MARKAHZI WILL BUILD ON THE LEGACY OF HOPELESSNESS YOU LEAVE BEHIND.*

Myles and his friends fly up from the hard granite floor and spin vertically in the air, suspended upside-down. He's still trying to catch his breath when he's in motion once more, smashed full force against the unforgiving cave wall. The clumps of blood-colored organic material press against the left side of his face. The slimy scoops of shimmering crimson slip through his lips, wiggle through the cracks in his teeth, and settle into his gums. It feels like scorpion stings on his tongue, leaving him with a bitter taste of rotten watermelon. Myles cannot express his displeasure, because he can't breathe, and his tongue is numb and vocal cords are paralyzed. The part of his brain that connects to his lungs is blocked, and he is seized with panic as he begins to suffocate.

Myles hears primitive grunts and squeals as the rest of the Friendly Forest Few huffs and puffs and struggles against the overwhelming telekinetic power of the Queen's will. While his brain and body are immobilized, his heart is not, and it pumps like a runaway train. Still upside-down, he feels his blood sinking from his legs down to his chest and cranium, alleviating some of the loopy sensation of asphyxiation. He realizes a lack of oxygen may put him out of his misery before gravity kills him.

The more Myles tries to shout with rage, the closer he comes to choking on his flaccid tongue. Seething with angst, he watches Kylie jiggle with futile resistance as the spawning material expands from the wall of the cave, unfolds into tiny worms that smother the back of her hair, and slide into her ear. The worms extend from the bloody goo on the granite's surface onto Myles's cheeks and slither into his eyes that he can no longer shut. Myles watches up close as the worms burrow into his pupils, and they create a crimson haze over his field of vision.

His perspective changes. No longer seeing the detailed expressions of the creepy crawlers conquering his face, but instead, his mind is removed from the agony of its defeat. He stands on his own two feet, surrounded by the majestic redwoods that once enshrined Camp Friendly Forest. He is surrounded by José, Tiffany, the expats, and other staff and children, lighter days far removed from the current turmoil.

The ground shakes playfully, the trees quiver joyfully, and for a moment they bask in a supernatural halo.

YOU INVITED US TO DESTROY YOU, the Queen blares in his mind, a disturbing voiceover to an otherwise positive memory.

Myles's view shifts again, this time to Earth a hundred miles above the atmosphere: a serene sphere with rippling white clouds, azure oceans, and lush tuffs of land set in galactic tranquility. From the northern border of modern-day Russia, a black, inky liquid spreads around the globe.

IT IS UNUSUAL IN THIS UNIVERSE, EVEN AMONG LOWER-LEVEL SPECIES, TO TERRAFORM A BIOSPHERE TO THE POINT THAT IT BECOMES UNINHABITABLE, YET HOMO SAPIENS HAVE MANAGED TO DO SO WITH AN ASTONISHING UNWILLINGNESS TO SAFEGUARD THEIR OWN SURIVIVAL. THE WARMING GASES BEING RELEASED INTO EARTH'S ATMOSPHERE HAVE DOOMED YOU AND YOUR PLANET'S LIFEFORMS TO AN EXTINCTION-LEVEL EVENT. THUS, THE HOME WORLD OF HOMO SAPIENS HAS BECOME A TARGET FOR

GALACTIC GENOCIDE AND A RIPE RESETTLEMENT ZONE FOR THE MARKAHZI.

The black ink covers Earth in a cloud of darkness, smothering the entire planet.

SOON THE WORST IMPACT OF YOUR TERRAFORMING WILL BE COMPLETE, AND THE MARKAHZI WILL TRANSFORM FROM A SPIRTUAL MANIFESTATION OF YOUR COLLECTIVE ILL WILL AND SUICIDAL TENDENCIES INTO A MATERIAL FORCE THAT TAKES POSSESSION OVER YOUR DYING RACE. AT LAST, WE WILL REVERT FROM A NANO GAS INFECTING YOUR MINDS AND ASSUME OUR TRUE FORM—

Demons that will create hell on Earth, José's mind projects.

They came to warn us about climate change, Tiffany adds, *then they stayed to live their best life.*

Her remark is followed by a round of telepathic laughter.

Parasitic thought-monsters gotta hustle for planetary domination, right? Tony projects, followed by more telepathic laughter.

Unless we change our minds, Kylie says, *and we roast this bad girl!*

The Queen has overstayed her fifteen minutes of fame, Myles adds. The affirmation of positive vibes flows through his and his peers' veins like a pot of coffee, supercharging their soul. *It's time to take back the mike and show this heckler off stage!*

Myles's backpack flaps open, and he feels a smooth silkiness slide down his neck, tugging onto his hair. As he wonders what new nightmarish creature has been unleashed upon them, the Friendly Forest Few are released from their gravitational hold. They drop to the granite floor, roll in sync into a forward summersault, and land on their feet in a fighting stance.

The Queen's eyes fill with fire. Her mouth opens wide, preparing to chew the youngsters to pieces, and her tail swerves, an over-sized whip snapping around her massive frame, knocking stalactites off the ceiling of the cave …

Myles feels something flopping around his leg. He glances toward the granite floor, surprised to find his childhood hero with an announcement to make.

"I – AM SUPERNOVA CID!"

Chapter 23

The rebel doll leaps across the cavern, locking onto the Queen's burning eyes.

"I COME FROM A MASSIVE BLACK HOLE IN THE CENTER OF THE GALAXY! WHY DO I MATTER? BECAUSE I *ATTRACT* MATTER!"

Myles and his peers gawk in amazement as the perturbed extraterrestrial thrashes, trying to shake off the figurine that disrupts her field of vision. The Friendly Forest Few uses her distraction to their advantage.

Attack! José yells, not in words, but as an image blasted into their minds.

In unison, they abandon their guns, withdraw their blades, and lunge toward the glittering monster. Together they scramble up the scales and plunge their axes and knives into her flesh. Myles's tomahawk cuts deep into the alien meat, his body dangling from the handle as the Queen emits a high-pitched sonic wave: *KA-CHUN-KA-TAY-LEEEEE!*

As foreign a sound as that is, her angry cry easily translates to their human ears. A blotchy, bile-like neon red fluid bursts from multiple stabbings in the belly of the beast. As the Queen writhes, tail swinging wildly, Tiffany telegraphs the next move. *Now!*

Gripping onto the handles of their blades, the Friendly Forest Few yank downward, each splitting the Queen's girth into five sections as their incisions glide them down to the ground.

CHI-KY-LA-TA! CHI KY-LA-TI-SA-NU-MEEEEE!

The Queen's agony is palpable. Alien blood gushes from the long slits, drowning the youngsters in putrid sludge while they slip, slide, and scramble to their feet. Myles flicks the beast's bodily fluids out of his eyes. There's a hideous snap, and a wall of golden viscera flashes toward them—

SMACK!

The tail launches them off the ground and smashes them back into the wall of granite. Myles feels his bones crack and the air blast out of his lungs, leaving him deflated. Kylie, José, Tony, and Tiffany pile onto the ground around him with lifeless thuds. In one whack, they are devastated. They have no more physical fight left. As they gasp for breath, and cling together in desperation, their eyes turn upward toward the white-hot phlegm dripping out from the nasty mama's mouth ...

"I VANQUISH MY ENEMIES THROUGH THE POWER OF ATTTRACTION!" Supernova Cid shouts, smothering the Queen with hugs and kisses. "LOVE IS LOVE—THE GREAT COSMIC EQUALIZER!"

Kylie's smooth, little fingers clasp Myles's right hand, and Tony's firm fingers clasp his left. Their touch triggers his grief, his tears flowing freely as blood pours from the Queen and pools around them.

Myles can't help but feel robbed. Not by fate, not by God, not even by aliens, but by himself. While his skepticism toward humanity seems to have been fair, such cynicism has prematurely aged him. In the blink of an eye, he realizes he has gone from being an awkward adolescent to a know-it-all adult. And the truth is, he never *hated* his life. He just felt overwhelmed by his powerlessness living in a world bent on destruction. So, he hid—in his bedroom, in the shadows, away from his better self. Like most of his generation, his nation, his species—his sensitivity fueled a trajectory of disdain, closing him off to a goodness that has always required more diligence, patience, and sacrifice to cultivate than hate.

I mean, I just graduated from high school, and the only woman I've ever kissed is my mother. I never snuck out at night and toilet-papered the homes of my enemies, because I was never bold enough to have real enemies, just as I never really had true friends. Until today.

Suddenly, everything Myles will *never* experience is a slash to his heart.

I long … to be in love!

The voices of his friends join him.

I long … to bake a cake!

I long … to drive a car!

I long … to cosplay at a comic con!

Their thoughts of hope spread like a virus. As the Friendly Forest Few reflects on the dreams they still have for their young lives, Supernova Cid, latched to the extraterrestrial matriarch, sparkles and shines. A series of florescent arcs spiral out from the doll's chest, brilliant streaks of light that resemble solar flares, bright and magnificent, mesmerizing and meaningful, a radiant spectacle that grows and expands and annihilates all within its sight.

Slumped together in the darkness, their hands clasped together, their bodies bruised and broken, the Friendly Forest Few watches with wonder as Supernova Cid explodes into a dazzling array of light. The Queen's eyes melt. Her razor-sharp teeth dissolve. As she, the cave, and the Friendly Forest few begin to wash away, Myles is eager to know the truth, voyage to new realms, and discover what awaits. As he and his friends disappear into the light, he recalls the insight of a fantasy book he once read—there are more worlds than this one.

The light fades, leaving them as they were less than a week ago. They stand beneath the towering shade of a redwood grove, counselors and campers struggling to resolve a silly, tribal conflict.

Geo approaches José, pointing at his chest. "What's it gonna take for you to keep your frick'n mouth shut?" he says, balling fingers into a fist, showing off the flecks of blood still covering his knuckles. "At this point, *homie*, I have nothing to lose."

José and Myles stare at each other. They know they should be angry. Here is Geo, an alpha predator trying to exert his dominance, but this time, reliving this moment, the young men could care less.

The situation, in the grand scheme of things, is laughable.

"Go screw a donut," José says with a shrug. "I've got bigger worries on my mind."

"Right," Myles says, giving his buddy a high-five.

"Excuse me?" Geo says, stepping closer to José.

"You heard him," Myles says, stepping closer to Geo. "Get lost and work on your daddy issues, dude. You don't have much time."

The expats shake their heads in collective agreement.

"Well said," Tony whispers to Myles, huddling close to his friends.

They exchange amused nods.

A sound, like a sonic boom, rattles the forest. The eyes of Myles, José, Geo, and the other counselors and campers turn upward. A gust of wind rushes through the redwoods, and a murder of crows burst from their perches in the branches, the black scavengers cawing noisily at each other as they scatter into the sky.

"Earthquake?" asks one of the expats.

A wave of shimmering light, a kaleidoscope of color immerses everything around them in a spectacle of beauty and warmth. It's unlike anything Myles has ever seen, like showering under a rainbow.

"Whoa," someone mutters.

The gust of wind dies, the birds are gone, and the consciousness-expanding light fades as quickly as it arrived. The impact of passing color, however, is something that Myles can only begin to imagine. *Something extraordinary is happening.*

This time, he is ready. Myles, José, and Tony exchange glances. They rush toward the crowd forming outside of the *Chill Room*. There they find Tiffany and Kylie waiting and ushering them inside: *Let's go!*

Together the Friendly Forest Few gazes at the spellbound onlookers and assesses the situation. Curtains are drawn and volumes run high on a row of monitors arranged on tables side by side. They display different channels, stations, and sites, the images flashing bits and pieces, clips and commentary, revolving around a developing news story.

At 2:35 p.m., a mile-long alien ship appeared from a wormhole that materialized outside Earth's atmosphere and discharged the massive freighter, which hurtled across the sky and crashed into the Pacific. Video footage taken from surfers congregating on a hill at a beach near Marine Corps Base Camp Pendleton, north of San Diego, shows vestiges of a tsunami wiping out a portion of the Interstate 5 Freeway, displacing cars and trucks, and dragging onto shore piles of seaweed, fish, and trash. A jarring scene follows consisting of blaring horns, mobilizing troops, and soldiers arresting the blond trespassers in wet suits as fighter jets scramble through clouds above toward the wrecked spaceship jutting out from the ocean.

But that's not why everyone is so excited. Seated at the far wall is a woman with a red hoodie, blond locks covering her face. The *Chill Room* is full of mirth, with counselors and campers taking pictures and recording her with their phones.

"Alice Walker!"

"Lady Prophet!"

"The psychic we read about in history books!"

"The one who predicted the '26 Earthquake!"

Seated next to the mysterious celebrity is a man, also in his late twenties. Myles recognizes the famous hacker. What's his name? *Henrik Gustavo.* Gus sits next to Alice Walker in a gray sweatshirt and jeans, absorbed in tech work, waving his empty hands dramatically before a computer screen as if summoning a dragon from cyberspace.

Alice finishes a drawing on scratch paper, leans back in her chair, props her sneakers on a table. With her caramel colored-skin and golden dreads, she is more stunning in person than the pics of her spammed across social media, Myles realizes. She points at the screens broadcasting its endless loop of terrible news.

"An alien invasion is underway," she says, her comments livestreaming, projecting on the computer monitors in the room. "These extraterrestrials look like wild dogs from outer space, and they are terrifying, playing off our collective fears, all based on a popular video game."

Sitting next to Myles is Billy. He glances up at his counselor with a vacant smile. Even as Alice speaks, and the nightmarish scenario of the *Kiaski* takeover unfolds on the net, Myles is not surprised to find Billy in this universe, or any other, glued to his game, preferring the comforts of virtual reality to a consensual one.

"This alien race recently ran a simulation to test our weaknesses, and by doing so, they also left a blueprint for their attack," Alice says, raising her map high for all to see. The map shows California, its southern half covered in red and marked EXTRATERRESTRIAL TERRITORY. "There were five survivors during this first wave of the invasion. Each of them is in this room with me now." She points again at the map. "The rest of you—all thirty million of you in range of this broadcast—probably don't remember dying. Because of the overwhelming fear and grief that you felt during the onslaught, you surrendered to the invaders, and your minds shut off and became fodder for the enemy. It was a collective hallucination to which you succumbed, spread through the air you breath. The only reason you're aware now is because of the five survivors."

Myles's stomach tightens as he hears the subtext of Alice's message: *The war is not over yet.*

"This extraterrestrial menace has adjusted their plan. In a week, their territory will expand, and they will consume the entire West Coast. In a month, North America. In a year, the whole planet. Most of humanity will perish over the course of Worlds War One. Those spared will serve as hosts for the alien race, which will repopulate Earth in their own image."

At that moment, Alice's escort, Gus, glances up at the crowd. On his forehead a lump appears, shifting back and forth, and a flap of skin lifts, revealing a third eye. There are gasps from campers and counselors. The black, ominous pupil surveys the room, detached from its host, peering at each person with a perplexed stare.

Jeanie shrieks. Geo shouts. Billy glances at the triclops, as if daydreaming, and resumes playing his video game.

"They call themselves the *Markahzi*, and we lured them to Earth with our overproduction of greenhouse gases," Alice says. "Our dying world will provide a perfect habitat for their new home." She gazes at the line of phones recording her prophesy. "But our demise need not be catastrophic, or complete. We can change the course of events. We can evolve and save our race. But to do so, we need help."

Her eyes pan the room, connecting one by one with each member of the Friendly Forest Few: José, Tiffany, Kylie, Tony and finally, Myles.

"So, what do you say?" she asks them. "Will you join me on a quest to liberate us from our alien overlords?"

"Before we agree," Myles says, stepping forward, hands resting on a table, "I have a question, Alice. If the hell my friends and I just went through was only a *simulation* in which we watched everyone around us *die*—" he gazes into the psychic's eyes. They sparkle like billions of stars, an expanding cosmos of optimism "—then how can we be sure that *this* reality … isn't another *simulation*?"

Billy and Jeanie and Geo and the rest of the counselors and campers packed into the *Chill Room* turn toward Myles and his friends. On each of their foreheads, a third eye awakens, black pupils staring at them.

In this crowd of cringy triclopses, Alice's unblemished forehead remains a pleasant relief. "Good question, Myles," she says, pressing Gus's forearm. She and he stand at attention. "That's why I am recruiting you and your friends, the Initiates, on this mission to save Earth—because I love the way you *think*."

THE END

Acknowledgements

Stories are created by storytellers, but they would die in an author's imagination if it weren't for those who support an author's work. In my case, I am grateful to the following individuals for helping me bring The Initiates to life:

- My wife, Jesse, and daughter, Sage, who inspired me to write a novel for a younger generation of readers.
- A.L. Lorentz and Liz Fine, two extraordinary writers whose feedback in the early stages of the manuscript were essential in shaping this story into the best one possible.
- Eric Sylvester, whose steady hand as a visual artist created the map by which readers might wander through extraterrestrial territory.
- The team at Between the Lines Publishing, who agreed with me that youth deserve stories that encourage them to think big about life's possibilities and their role for the future.

RYAN HYATT tells stories about your future. He is a former news reporter and columnist, and he is a current educator and author of the Terrafide series. Ryan edits the satirical sci-fi news site, The La-La Lander, as well as Not Your Father's Bedtime Stories, kid's lit he creates with his daughter, author Sage Hyatt. Find him at the beach and his stories across the internet. Connect with him @ucalthisreality.

www.ingramcontent.com/pod-product-compliance
Lightning Source LLC
Chambersburg PA
CBHW010751310726
48974CB00004B/877